THE DOYLE DIARY

THE LAST GREAT CONAN DOYLE MYSTERY

WITH A HOLMESIAN INVESTIGATION
INTO THE STRANGE AND CURIOUS CASE OF
CHARLES ALTAMONT DOYLE

BY MICHAEL BAKER

PADDINGTON PRESS LTD

NEW YORK & LONDON

Thank you for hiding this book at the store so I could get it for you. Much love, Gloria 2-14-'83

Library of Congress Cataloging in Publication Data
Doyle, Charles Altamont
    The Doyle Diary

    Facsim. of the author's diary-sketchbook, with an additional introd.
    I.   Doyle, Charles Altamont   II.   Artists—England—Biography
I.   Baker, Michael, 1948-   II.   Title.
N6797.D68A2 1978   741'.092'4 (B)   78-6356
ISBN 0 7092 0047 1
ISBN 0 448 22068 7 (US & Canada only)

Typeset in England by Whitecross Graphics Ltd., London
Produced by Mohn-Gordon Limited, London and
    printed in Germany by Mohndruck Gütersloh
Color separations by Starf Photo Lito, Rome, Italy
Designed by Colin Lewis

In the United States PADDINGTON PRESS Distributed by GROSSET & DUNLAP

In the United Kingdom PADDINGTON PRESS

In Canada Distributed by RANDOM HOUSE OF CANADA LTD.

In Southern Africa Distributed by ERNEST STANTON (PUBLISHERS) (PTY.) LTD.

CONTENTS

Charles Doyle and the 6-year-old Arthur (Edinburgh, 1865)

INTRODUCTION

THE STRANGE AND CURIOUS CASE OF
CHARLES ALTAMONT DOYLE

BY MICHAEL BAKER

"My dear fellow," said Sherlock Holmes, as we sat on either side of the fire in his lodgings at Baker Street, "life is infinitely stranger than anything which the mind of man could invent."

So BEGINS ONE of the first short stories Arthur Conan Doyle wrote about the exploits of his great detective. Its title, appropriately enough, was "A Case of Identity," and this, as well as the sentiment expressed in its opening sentence, would have made a fitting introduction to the tale which surrounds this bizarre and original book. For fiction could not have conceived of a more singular set of circumstances than those which went to make up the true-life story of Charles Altamont Doyle.

Hitherto almost nothing was known about Doyle beyond the fact that he was the father of the celebrated writer of detective fiction. Now the discovery of this strange volume has suddenly afforded a glimpse at an existence behind the name – but one that seems at first so tenuous and distant that even the legendary Baker Street sleuth would probably have found the case a trifle baffling. Indeed, so compelling are the known details of the matter, so tantalizingly elusive is the central character in the drama, and – not least – so utterly ironic is it that the creator of Sherlock Holmes should himself be party to an unexplained mystery on his own doorstep, that it is impossible to resist giving some account of it, however speculative.

Doyle's book first came to light in early 1977. It belonged to an Englishwoman who had been given it more than twenty years before by a friend who had in turn bought it in a job lot of books at a house sale in the New Forest. This was probably

Bignell House, Conan Doyle's country retreat near Minstead, which was sold by the Doyle family in 1955. For years the book lay undisturbed, stored with other items in a children's playroom. But finally, on the recommendation of a painter friend, its owner approached the Maas Gallery with it. The Maas Gallery, one of the leading dealers in Victorian art in London, quickly realized that the Doyle book was a major find. Richard or "Dicky" Doyle, Charles's brother, had long been familiar to art historians as a talented and successful Victorian illustrator, but only in the previous ten years had there been any awareness of Charles—and even then only through rare individual works. Here, however, was evidence for the first time of a more systematic output which, in its scope and originality, entitled Charles to artistic status in his own right.

The appearance of Doyle's book marked the beginning of a sort of personal odyssey for me. I was shown the work in the summer of 1977 and was instantly intrigued. It seemed to exercise a strange attraction, rather like looking at one's image in the still depths of a forest pool. Doyle's artistic merit I was incapable of judging properly, but this did not matter. What struck me forcibly about his weird and delicate pictures was the vivid impression they created of time and place and personality. None of these elements was well defined, and yet this in no way lessened the book's impact; rather it was the very intangibility of the presence pervading the sketches which stirred my curiosity. Moreover, the bizarre circumstances in which the artist had apparently worked excited the imagination with all manner of Gothic fantasies. In short, the more I studied the book the more I was gripped by its mysteries, the

more I was fascinated by the man behind the artist. It was not so much a who-dunnit as a who-was-it. Who *was* Charles Doyle? The question nagged at the corners of the mind, the book before me assuming quite as great an urgency as any corpse lying at my feet in a pool of blood. There was nothing for it. I resolved to turn detective, to sleuth out the truth, gumshoeing my way down the cobwebbed corridors of history, knocking on its doors and questioning the occupants within, searching for those telltale fingerprints which would identify the suspect, and finally handcuffing him in the manacles of descriptive prose. It went without saying that Sherlock Holmes would serve as my model.

The book of sketches was, like the body under the floorboards, my only clue. It didn't seem much to go on. Its curiosities appeared at first to obscure the identity of the artist rather than reveal it. Yet I recalled that it was an axiom of Holmes's that, as a rule, the more bizarre a thing is the less mysterious it proves to be. And so it was in this case on closer inspection.

The book was less fruitful now as evidence than it once might have been, for many of the penciled annotations among the drawings had faded out or been erased. But examination yielded several straightforward deductions and a few others which were based upon strong probability. It was plain, for instance, that Charles Doyle was Irish, and a staunch patriot at that; that he was a devout Catholic, middle-aged, tall, slight, with a long beard; and that he suffered from shortsightedness. He was possessed of considerable wit and learning. He obviously adored his wife, who parted her hair in the center.

He knew Edinburgh well, had once kept cats, and had an intimate knowledge of heraldry. Holmes would have had no quarrel with my technique so far, and I began to perceive the real value of his methods. I pushed my deductions further. Though resident in a lunatic asylum, Doyle was clearly not mad, but was subject to headaches and prolonged periods of depression. He had a distinct penchant for puns and whimsy, appeared to be afraid of birds, believed in fairies, and was of an unworldly and careless disposition.

No Holmes is without his Watson, and my own jumped in at this juncture with cries of incredulity. But I had to assure him that the matter was elementary; that although the evidence lay before his very eyes, he was failing to reason from what he saw. In the first place, there were extensive notes penciled in Doyle's neat handwriting on many pages which made the sketchbook something of a private journal as well—a not inconsiderable record, in fact, of his varying moods from day to day as the inmate of an insane asylum (referred to as "Sunny-side") in the year 1889. From his jottings it appeared that Doyle was far from happy at his detention in this institution or with the consequent imputation that he was mad. Indeed, he was offering his work as evidence of his sanity. "Keep steadily in view," he had written on the first page, "that this Book is ascribed wholly to the produce of a MADMAN. Where-abouts would you say was the deficiency of intellect? or de-praved taste?" And on page 56, reflecting upon the commercial potential of his "many Vols of . . . not serious Work" (suggest-ing, incidentally, that other sketchbooks existed), he stated his belief that it was only the "Scotch Misconception of Jokes"

which branded him as mad. Indeed, only a sane man, and a clever one at that, could have added the rider that "many things are best expressed by stating what they are not—as for instance my claim for Sanity is not best made by enlarging on my common sense." As it happened, such a principle was perhaps not the wisest to act upon in Doyle's case, but here was a man who clearly had his wits about him and who, by contrast with another "mad" fairy painter, Richard Dadd,* had retained a strong sense of his professional worth in the outside world. If Doyle's own account is to be believed, it was not a conviction shared by either his family (by whom he felt deserted) or the medical authorities.

But if Doyle was not mad, the pages of his book did reveal a man of melancholic disposition (perhaps understandable in the circumstances), given to bouts of depression, neurosis and morbidity. His devout Catholicism, evident in recollections of his childhood (page 15) and allusions to the Ursulines (page 47), combined with this condition to produce an almost obsessive preoccupation with death, especially death as a deliverance from his fate. This was captured with the greatest poignancy in his drawing "Well Met" (page 55), where he humbly greets the skeletal, scythe-carrying figure of Death ("I do believe that to a Catholic there is Nothing so sweet in life as leaving it," reads the caption), and in another (page 72), where the artist is depicted "BUSTING OUT" of imprisoning Life and regaining his freedom. As for his Irishness, well, Doyle is an Irish name, but there were frequent allusions to the "Irish Question" in the book, usually conveying a sense of outrage at

*Dadd was committed to Bethlem Hospital after murdering his father in 1843.

British treatment of the Irish (pages 15, 26 and 46). There was also a design drawing for a memorial to the Irish patriot Lord Edward Fitzgerald murdered in 1798 (page 21).

"Come, come, my dear fellow, this is all very well," broke in the attentive Watson at my shoulder, "but what about the headaches and the prolonged depression? Surely this is a matter for medical records not deducible here. And how on earth can you tell what Doyle looks like?"

"My dear Watson, you refuse to believe the evidence of your own eyes," I retorted, "for these clues are the most glaring of all."

The headaches were easily settled. Doyle referred to "a tremendous headach [sic]" on May 22, 1889, and made it the occasion for several puns at his own expense (pages 40-41); he also alluded (page 30) to the ministering powers of Mrs. Brewster "when a headach wrings the brow." It was anyway not medically implausible that a patient of his depressive disposition would suffer from headaches.

The prolonged nature of his depressions required rather greater concentration. As I compared the dates on the drawings, I could see that on at least two occasions Doyle's thoughts on death and his sense of grievance at his detention continued for several consecutive days. On June 5, 1889, he was lamenting the fact that the authorities had seen fit to "endorse utterly false conceptions of sanity or insanity to the detriment of the life and liberty of a harmless gentleman" (page 56). On June 6 he seemed happy enough at a country picnic; but on June 7 his depression was worse than ever and he had a wild premonition of his own death which was accompanied, on the one hand,

by a sudden burst of affection for his wife and children and, on the other, by a sense of tranquillity at the thought that he was passing to his real home at last (pages 47 and 72). Similarly, on both July 18 and 19 (pages 60 and 76), he was preoccupied with joining Death and "Being Taken Up" ("I hope so," was his comment in the margin).

Indeed, the dates suggested something more to me about Doyle. They were scattered at random throughout the book in no particular order, some of the earlier ones coming at the back, some of the later nearer the front. In other words, the artist appeared to have sketched haphazardly through his book with little concern to fill it up consecutively, page by page. This implied an artistic, undisciplined temperament, if not a careless one, and taking into account a subject matter which concentrated heavily upon flora, fauna and fairies (his skill at drawing plants and flowers denoted an expert naturalist), it did not seem to be stretching the bounds of probability too far to conclude that our artist had more of the visionary and dreamer in him than the practical man of affairs.

But did he really believe in fairies? Well, it was certainly not inconceivable given his artistic obsession with them, and the notion was lent added weight by two scribbled comments: one beside a sprig of chestnut which read "I have seen a green lad just like it" (page 22); the other under a pen-and-ink study of a "cat-girl" with the words "I have known such a creature" (page 28). Both remarks are admittedly ambiguous, but I was led to wonder whether Doyle's fondness for the supernatural did not merely confirm his doctors' opinion of his health. Equally, if he had simply been pursuing his own policy of abnegating common sense to demonstrate his sanity, it did not seem to be a very successful course of action.

As for the artist's appearance, that was simple. He had executed self-portraits in several places. The best was on page 7, where he self-deprecatingly drew himself as "A HEAVY SWELL," a whimsical reference perhaps to his plumpness here (though elsewhere he was generally thin and fragile). His large head, small rimless glasses and long beard lent him an academic air, and indeed his enthusiasm for excruciating puns and comic riddles was distinctly donnish at times (some of the most typical examples are to be found on page 4). The spectacles suggested shortsightedness, and this was confirmed on page 30 where he admitted he was too shortsighted to catch Mrs. Brewster's likeness well.

As to his wife and his adoration, both were graphically depicted in a rather pathetic sketch showing Doyle gazing with the fond admiration of a small boy up at his wife Mary. "MY IDEAL HOME RULER," he commented in a caption which slyly alluded to the Irish question (page 27). This drawing confirmed the identity of a woman with an oval face, center parting and swept-back hair who frequently cropped up in the book.

For the rest, the sketches told their own story plainly enough. Edinburgh? No artist unfamiliar with the city would have located the procession of heralds on page 53 quite so precisely. His delight in heraldic symbols could hardly be missed: the lion and the unicorn on the royal coat of arms was a special favorite of his as a vehicle for a whole string of puns and wisecracks (pages 2 and 44). That he kept cats was also

easy to tell: there was one drawn in a curious domestic scene on page 60 and a more explicit one, draped around the artist's shoulders, on page 71 over the caption "WHERE PUSSY USED TO SIT AT HOME." With Charles Doyle's fear of birds I was perhaps intruding on the territory of the psychoanalyst, but it was surely not without significance that almost all the birds he had drawn (and some other wild creatures such as squirrels and polecats) were abnormally large, even for fairies, and frequently assumed rather threatening attitudes; indeed, his fairies spent a lot of time interceding with these predators of the air on behalf of more vulnerable creatures such as worms and butterflies (pages 14 and 17).

So, for all of the book's quaint mysteries, indeed because of them, it was possible at once to discern an identifiable human being—of necessity a rather skeletal being, but nevertheless decidedly human. This did not make the case an open and shut one, as my Watsonian companion would have had it. Far from it. For if the Sunnyside journal had yielded a surprising number of clues to Doyle's character and condition (and not least to his psychological state of mind), it was conspicuously limited as a piece of evidence pointing to the artist's wider circumstances.

In this area probability shaded off sharply into mere conjecture. It was true, coherent glimpses of life in an asylum cut across an otherwise jumbled mass of ideas, and Doyle's personal experience—sketching, walks, picnics and "pick-me-ups"—suggested that his own conditions were relatively peaceful and relaxed (though no doubt his self-absorption exaggerated this impression.) But overall the work was too internalized, too much a reflection of the artist's inner dream world, to provide intelligible clues to his objective position in the world. Reality obtruded but rarely into the patchwork of jocularity and fantasy, and where it did the world of the institution, with its gaunt gables, dormitories and polished floors (doctors and nurses are strangely absent), hid our gaze from the less comfortable world outside. Only once, where Charles reproduced some press reviews of *Micah Clarke* and *The Mystery of Cloomber* (page 28), did I get any inkling that this was the father of the famous son. And what was to be made of passing remarks like "would I could hide my other deficiencies!" on page 13 or captions such as "PREVENTION IS BETTER THAN CURE" (page 23) and "THE DREADFUL SECRET," a haunting sketch of great dramatic power (page 37)? Above all, the sketches supplied no answer to the most provoking questions of all: What was a man of Doyle's apparent lucidity, albeit eccentric at times, doing in a Scottish lunatic asylum against his will? How long had he been there? What was his life beforehand? And how did all this tie up with Arthur Conan Doyle?

Had I really been Sherlock Holmes, I might at this juncture have sat for some time in silence with my head sunk forward, my eyes bent upon the red glow of the embers, my fingertips together in an attitude of prayer. I would then have lit a pipe and, leaning back in the chair, would have watched as the blue smoke rings chased each other up the wall to the ceiling. Holmes would have set it out rather like this. Once the ideal reasoner has been shown a fact in all its bearings, he should be able to deduce from it not only the whole chain of events leading up to it, but also all the consequences that would follow. Rather as Cuvier, the early nineteenth-century French anatomist, could correctly describe a whole animal by examining a single bone. In this way, problems which had baffled more practical lines of investigation could be solved in the study.

To carry this art to its highest perfection, however, the reasoner must have possession of all the facts likely to be useful to him. In the case of Charles Doyle, it was clear that the bearings were lacking. As yet I had no intelligible context in which the book could be placed, and it was in this direction that my enquiries would now have to turn. The one certain fact known about the Sunnyside artist was that he was Conan Doyle's father. Plainly, the next step in the search for clues lay with the life of the celebrated author.

Leaving aside the voluminous writings devoted to Conan Doyle's fiction (most of it about the Holmes stories), the field narrowed to a dozen or so proper biographical studies of the writer, some of them very recent. It must be said that a scrupulous rummaging in these works did little to lift the veil of obscurity around Charles. Indeed, not a few I found carelessly researched, repetitive of earlier writings and over-eager to speculate with modern hindsight where the facts wore thin. So if in Charles's case an outline of a life now began to emerge, I still had difficulties recognizing a flesh-and-blood personality.

I learned from the biographies that Charles Altamont Doyle was born in 1832 and died in 1893 at the age of 61. His father, John Doyle, whose family originated from Dublin, was the celebrated political caricaturist of the Regency period known under the pseudonym of "HB." His mother was Marianna Conan, the sister of Michael Conan, an artist, critic and journalist working on both sides of the Channel. His elder brother, Dicky Doyle (born 1824), acquired a considerable reputation as an illustrator, notably for *Punch* in the 1840s (the best-known title page of the magazine, still in use well into this century, was Dicky's work). Charles had three other brothers: Francis, who died at an early age after showing great promise as an artist; and James and Henry, both talented artists who reached positions of eminence in later life. James was a scholarly man and made a reputation with his illustrated *Chronicles of England* (1864) and the massive *Official Baronage of England* (1885), which took him thirteen years to complete and became an authoritative textbook of the College of Arms. His best known painting is *A Literary Party at Sir Joshua Reynolds's*. Henry began as a painter and art critic, and was commissioned to execute the murals of the Last Judgment in the Roman Catholic Church at Lancaster. In 1869 he was appointed director of the National Gallery of Ireland which, under his guidance, acquired many Dutch and Flemish paintings. He was subsequently made a Companion of the Bath.

Such a talented brood inevitably attracted attention and the family home in Cambridge Terrace, Hyde Park, was the frequent resort of the early Victorian generation of artistic and literary luminaries, among them Thackeray, Rosetti, Millais and Landseer. But in reality the Doyles were not great socialites, preferring a secluded and austere existence. John

One of the decorative initials that Charles's brother Dicky designed for Punch *in the 1840s. Both brothers were fascinated by the dreamlike world of the supernatural.*

Doyle (who had spent his honeymoon at Arundel Castle, home of the Duke of Norfolk, first Catholic peer of the realm) had brought up his family as strict Catholics, and none of them betrayed their faith. James's tall, stooping figure, black beard and pensive expression had earned him the nickname of "The Priest," and when Arthur Conan Doyle later proclaimed himself an agnostic, it was James who remained the foremost obstacle to any rapprochement between the writer and his uncles. Henry was a close friend of Cardinal Wiseman, whose portrait he painted (it now hangs in the National Gallery of Ireland), whereas Dicky resigned from his brilliant career with *Punch* in 1850 on account of the magazine's opposition to Pope

Pius IX's plan to establish a regular diocesan hierarchy in England, a move which outraged Anglicans.

But this rigid adherance to Catholicism (a suspect religion in England well into the nineteenth century) did not seem to have held back the talented Doyles. As Adrian Conan Doyle was at pains to point out in his biography of his father, *The True Conan Doyle* (1945), Arthur and his immediate forebears were "the only family in the British Empire to have given in the space of three generations five separate members" to the Dictionary of National Biography.

Charles Doyle's name was not among them. Like his brothers, he had also been trained as an artist, but success eluded him. In 1849, at the relatively young age of 17, he had been sent to Edinburgh to take up a post as assistant to the surveyor in the Scottish Office of Works, by all accounts a position of some responsibility, entailing the skills of architect, draftsman and builder. The move from London was apparently not a welcome one for Charles, but six months after his arrival he met the young Mary Foley, whom he eventually married in 1855. She was also Irish and Catholic, and the couple proceeded to have ten children, seven of whom survived (Arthur, the fourth child but first boy, was born in 1859). Charles seemed to make no particular mark in his new job, where he stayed put for the rest of his working life. He was supposed to have designed the fountain at Holyrood Palace in Edinburgh and one of the great windows in Glasgow Cathedral. His salary never rose above £250 (though book illustration in his spare time provided a little extra income), and family life was reputedly a struggle to make ends meet. It did not help that

Charles's health soon began to deteriorate; by the 1880s he had apparently retired and was resident in a "convalescent home."

This was the essence of the evidence on Charles in the Conan Doyle biographies. It was decidedly sketchy. It did help explain and corroborate many aspects suggested by the Sunnyside book, notably his religous devotion and his Irishness. The *Punch*-like sense of humor, and indeed the fantastical character of his artistic imagination, showed the influence of his successful brother Dicky, much of whose illustrative work, particularly his *Journal* (done as a boy but not published till 1885), *Dick Kitcat's Book of Nonsense* (1842), *The King of the Golden River* (1850), and *In Fairyland* (1870) depicted the same feverish visions and dreamlike world of the supernatural which inhabited Charles's art.* A sketched portrait by Dicky of Mary Foley gave added confirmation of the identity of the Mary in the sketchbook. Further, Charles's knowledge of heraldry now revealed its family roots. If James Doyle was something of an expert on the subject, Mary Foley, with her love of genealogy, was an ideal addition to a family fiercely proud of its Celtic ancestry (she was related to the Percys of Northumberland and was fond of tracing her ancestry back to the Plantagenets). As Adrian Conan Doyle recalled in *The True Conan Doyle*, Arthur's love for historical romance (viz. *The White Company*, *Rodney Stone*, *Micah Clarke* and *Sir Nigel*) thus owed much to an early acquaintance with the

* *Dicky also painted a number of canvasses on this theme, notably* The Witches' Home *and* Wood Elves Watching a Lady (*both in the Victoria and Albert*), *and* The Triumphant Entry—A Fairy-Tale Pageant (*National Gallery of Ireland*).

Mary, Charles's wife (sketch by Dicky Doyle)

Arthur, Charles's famous son (1892)

"chivalric sciences of the fifteenth century in the bosom of a family to whom pride of lineage was of an infinitely greater importance than the discomforts of that comparative poverty that had come to surround them."

As for Charles's character, the biographies, some containing a rare photograph of the artist showing a gentle face with a far-away expression, strengthened the impression suggested by a study of the Sunnyside book. He was variously described as "anemic," "melancholy and morbid," "dreamy and remote," "apathetic" and "naturally philosophic." He came to terms with life and its disappointments easily, retreating increasingly from both into himself. His family was distressed to see him give away work (which might have brought in much-needed extra income) rather than haggle over a decent price. The process of disintegration had begun.

In his *Life of Sir Arthur Conan Doyle* (1949) John Dickson Carr gives a fitting description of Charles at this time: "He loved fishing, because when you fished the nagging world let you alone. To his family he was becoming a dreamy, long-bearded stranger, with exquisite manners and an unbrushed top hat. Each day he trudged the long walk from home to his office at Holyrood Palace, and back again to pat the children's heads absent-mindedly, as he might have stroked his pet cats."

"Charles Doyle was neither a bad husband nor a bad father," wrote Pierre Nordon in the *Sir Arthur Conan Doyle Centenary* edition (1959). "Yet he was but little interested in his own family. . . . He was an egotist who could not be disturbed by his relations' need for confidence and communication, the very pattern of the bachelor tied in matrimony."

But despite the considerable light shed upon Doyle by his son's biographers, I was puzzled by a number of questions and discrepancies. On the surface it seemed obvious that here was a talented artist who was unable to face up to the disappointments of exile in Edinburgh, a humdrum civil servant's job and the demands of a large family; he had simply physically and mentally deteriorated under the strain. Yet, as Holmes would have been quick to point out, nothing is more deceptive than the obvious. None of this explained why Doyle was sent to Edinburgh at such a tender age in the first place. For a

family of such prominence, was this the best and the nearest opening they could find? Moreover, what exactly was his job and what were the circumstances of his departure from it? What was the true state of his condition which necessitated retirement to a "convalescent home"? I had been able to deduce that Doyle's health was probably beginning to give anxiety at the time Arthur was leaving school in 1875, and it was generally agreed by the biographers that he had entered a nursing home by 1879. But what was the matter with him? Was the "home" also an asylum? Was it Sunnyside, indeed? Above all, why had such a promising artistic talent of undeniable skill and originality, surrounded by a family of reputation and influence, never received an equal share of the world's recognition?

The biographies had remained obstinately vague, even those which had had the advantage of full access to the Conan Doyle correspondence.* A retiring and diffident personality was surely not sufficient explanation in itself for such a glaring exception to the uniform success and brilliance of the other Doyles. Indeed nobody had denied that Charles had talent. As Michael and Mollie Hardwick put it in *The Man Who Was Sherlock Holmes* (1964), Charles was "a brilliant artist . . . a master of fantasy in the Fuseli manner, able to create visions in line and color which contrived to be at the same time beautiful, haunting and disturbing." "Charles Doyle was an artist that never got his due," concluded another biographer, the Reverend John Lamond in *Arthur Conan Doyle: A Memoir*

*John Dickson Carr, The Life of Sir Arthur Conan Doyle (1949) and Pierre Nordon, Conan Doyle (1966).

(1931). "His genius was altogether remarkable.... [His pictures] are more weird than anything Blake ever produced." Fuseli? Blake? These were big names. Why not Doyle then? The case was turning into quite a three-pipe problem.

I found that the comparison between Charles Doyle and Blake had first been made by Arthur Conan Doyle in his autobiography *Memories and Adventures*, published in 1924. That same year he organized a London exhibition of some fifty of Charles's works (George Bernard Shaw thought the paintings deserved a room to themselves in any national gallery). Arthur had always considered his father the greatest artist in the family. "His work," he observed, "had a peculiar style of its own, mitigated by great natural humor. He was more terrible than Blake and less morbid than Wiertz. His originality is best shown by the fact that one hardly knows with whom to compare him."

The son's judgment of the father had not always been so admiringly filial. In the face of Charles's growing incapacity, it had been Arthur who had had to shoulder the burden of the large Doyle family and this had obliged him to work his way through college as a medical student. The memory had undoubtedly rankled. In the semi-autobiographical *Stark Munro Letters* (1894), an account of Conan Doyle's early experiences as a young doctor, the narrator recalls his father (who is "disguised" as a country GP with a "touch of gout") telling him that he suffered from a terminal illness which did not give him long to live and that it was a son's duty to find reliable employment as quickly as possible to support the family:

Of course I could only answer that I was willing to turn my hand to anything. But that interview has left a mark upon me—a heavy ever-present gloom away at the back of my soul, which I am conscious of even when the cause of it has for a moment gone out of my thoughts. I had enough to make man serious before, when I had to face the world without money or interest. But now to think of my mother and my sisters and little Paul all leaning upon me when I cannot stand myself—it is a nightmare.

There was no doubt that Conan Doyle had been far closer to his mother – "the quaintest mixture of the housewife and the woman of letters, with the high-bred spirited lady as a basis for either character" – and had probably resented his father's weakness and indifference. In his *Conan Doyle* (1966), Nordon suggested that the violence of Arthur's breach with the Doyle uncles over the question of religion derived in some way from a latent hostility to Charles, whose lack of warmth and determination contrasted so strongly with the radiant strength of his mother's personality. Nordon found it remarkable that Charles had made no attempt to prevent Arthur from rejecting Catholicism. In the *Stark Munro Letters*, however, there was evidence of considerable friction between father and son on the subject:

I fear there is little intellectual sympathy between us. He appears to think that those opinions of mine upon religion and politics which came from my inmost soul have been assumed either out of indifference or bravado. So I ceased to talk on vital subjects with him, and, though we affect to ignore it, we both know that there is a barrier there.

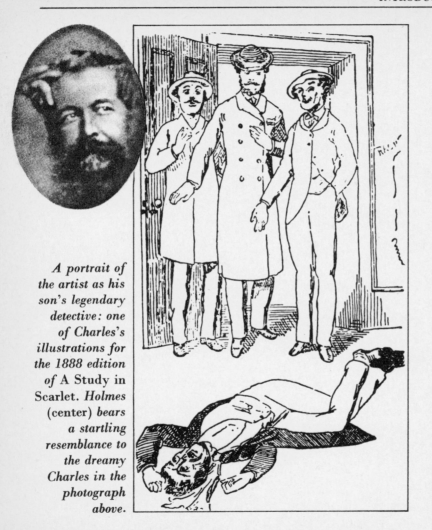

A portrait of the artist as his son's legendary detective: one of Charles's illustrations for the 1888 edition of A Study in Scarlet. Holmes *(center) bears a startling resemblance to the dreamy Charles in the photograph above.*

By the time Conan Doyle came to write *Memories and Adventures*, his attitude to his father had softened. As early as 1888, Charles had furnished six pen-and-ink drawings for the Ward Lock edition of *A Study in Scarlet*, the first full-length Sherlock Holmes novel (and, strikingly, had depicted a Holmes far removed from the Sidney Paget stereotype, presenting instead a figure not unlike himself). Arthur's recollection had now become an essentially affectionate one, which sought to praise and excuse rather than criticize. In so doing I realized it shed a rather different light on Charles's elusive character. He was, Arthur had recalled,

a tall man, long-bearded, and elegant; he had a charm of manner and courtesy of bearing which I have seldom seen equalled. His wit was quick and playful. He possessed, also, a remarkable delicacy of mind which would give him moral courage enough to rise and leave any company which talked in a manner which was coarse. . . . He was unworldly and impractical and his family suffered for it.

But even these faults, said Arthur, derived from a "developed spirituality."

All of a sudden I found myself looking at a different Charles Doyle. The melancholy neurotic of the biographers had been transformed, Jekyll-like, into a sensitive soul of charm and elegance. This begged an important question. Had Charles Doyle's character too often been deduced from the depressed and absent-minded figure that he later became? As I had seen earlier, Charles's Sunnyside book tended to suggest such a personality, yet even there I now had to admit that many of the drawings had radiated a wit and exuberance that were all the more striking for their contrast with the general tenor of anguish and morbidity.

In John Dickson Carr's biography of Conan Doyle, a very different picture of the young Charles in his first twenty years in Edinburgh emerged by comparison with the standard treatments. In his letters home, many of them embellished with pen-and-ink sketches, he had displayed every sign of youthful optimism and curiosity. He bubbled with ideas for new designs, avidly explored Edinburgh, and was roused to the heights of patriotic fervor by Queen Victoria's visit to the city in the summer of 1850 (Charles helped supervise the raising of the flag on the roof of Holyrood Palace, where his office was then situated). In these early years he had still cared. He wanted Arthur to become a businessman, and he cherished ideas of moving back to London or, with the help of Dicky's influence in high places, securing promotion in the Office of Works. Failing that, he might emigrate to Australia to dig for gold. It was not to be. Doyle was to remain in Edinburgh for the rest of his career. When he left finally, it was for the unwelcome confines of an institution.

It rather began to look as if Charles really had undergone a gradual change of personality. He had clearly not always been the thoroughgoing neurotic and depressive whom most of Arthur's biographers had singled out. Too often, in fact, writers have had a tendency, in the absence of dramatic facts, to scour Conan Doyle's fiction for clues to Charles's character (a practice restricted not only to Charles's case, it might be added, for few authors can have had so much read into their real lives from their fiction as Conan Doyle). Charles's spirit

was suddenly detectable in every story which produced an invalid or highly strung neurotic. Professor Gilroy, for example, the central figure in *The Parasite* (1894), Conan Doyle's macabre novella about mesmerism, was, according to one writer, "reminiscent not only of Sherlock Holmes but of Collins's *Woman in White*, and, of course, of the unhappy Charles Doyle."* Such heterogeneous parallels seemed to deny the point almost at once. It is true that Gilroy was "sensitive" and "highly psychic," but there was surely little similarity between Charles and a man who declared he had trained himself "to deal only with fact and with proof" and who eschewed "surmise and fancy." Elsewhere the same writer suggested that Charles was the inspiration behind the delirious narrator of *The Silver Mirror*, the story of a man experiencing a gradual nervous breakdown, as well as the source for Holmes's drug addiction, allegedly drawn from the sedative treatment Doyle would have undergone in his "nursing home." "Significantly," the writer confided mysteriously, "Holmes's drug taking would cease in 1896, three years after Charles Doyle's death." Significant indeed! It was no surprise, in fact, to find that this author saw part of Holmes *as* Charles Doyle, for like him, "he is remote and puzzling, alternating bursts of manic creative energy with long periods of exhaustion and isolation."†

It was impossible to take such loose speculation seriously. Nothing is easier than to go on indefinitely recreating Charles Doyle in the image of his son's fictional characters, seeing him,

Charles Higham, The Adventures of Conan Doyle (*1976*).
†Ibid, *pp. 70-71.*

say, in Lord Saltire's depressive son (in the *Stark Munro Letters*) or as the model for the bogus Russian count suffering from catalepsy in "The Resident Patient." Holmes himself would never have approved of such undisciplined methods of investigation.

Circumstantial evidence is a tricky matter, as the great detective was fond of remarking. It might seem to point very straight in one direction, but it only required the slightest shift of perspective to find it pointing equally decisively in an entirely different direction. I found this advice salutary when reviewing the evidence in the Conan Doyle biographies which bore on the case of Charles Doyle. To the casual observer, as I have mentioned, these works had built up a coherent picture of a disillusioned talent in decline. Yet what struck me about all of them* was their reticence to define Charles's ultimate disintegration, a disintegration indeed that was so marked that he had ended his days in a mental institution. Vague references to the artist's "declining health" simply did not square with the existence of evidence which proclaimed in unambiguous terms his involuntary detention in an asylum. In other words, the biographies appeared, from a different viewpoint, to raise more questions about the biographers and their methods than to supply answers about Charles Doyle. I was sure I had stumbled on something of real importance here. In one sense, it highlighted perhaps a genuine ignorance

*The one exception is Charles Higham's The Adventures of Conan Doyle (1976). Without saying how, Higham reaches the same conclusions as I do about Charles Doyle's medical condition, but I should point out that I did not read his book until after completing my own investigation.

or indifference about Charles, which was perhaps excusable in a biography of his son. Yet was such an omission equally justified in the case of those authors who were privileged to study the complete family papers, many of them relevant to the years between Charles Doyle's "retirement" and his death?

Conan Doyle himself, it seemed to me, was decidedly vague about his father's decline. In the *Stark Munro Letters* Charles was the least identifiable figure, and Conan Doyle gave him a heart condition to account for his gradual withdrawal from the scene. So far as is known, a bad heart has never qualified a man for a lunatic asylum. Thirty years later the famous writer was no more forthcoming, but his attempts to rehabilitate his father's memory left an impression not just of youthful judgments mellowed by age but of a determination to vindicate a life which had been, to all intents and purposes, a failure—and not merely for reasons of ill health.

In this connection, both the London exhibition of 1924 and Conan Doyle's own flirtation with fairies at this time were suggestive of a new significance. Arthur had always been interested in the occult, and after the First World War he took up spiritualism as a serious cause. He even claimed to have made spiritual contact with his father and other deceased members of his family on several occasions. By the end of his life, Conan Doyle had written a dozen books and many newspaper articles on life after death, and had lectured on the subject throughout the world. He eventually became President of the World Federation of Spiritualists.

But what really caught my attention was the fact that in 1922 Conan Doyle had produced an extraordinary book entitled *The Coming of the Fairies*. Here he had taken up and examined a number of cases where people had claimed not only to have seen fairies but to have photographed them as well. Perhaps the most striking of these was the case of two young Yorkshire girls from Cottingley who produced photos of themselves in the company of fairies and wood elves (the latter suitably attired in conventional pantomime costumes). Despite the marked ambiguity of the evidence as to the genuineness of the photographs, Conan Doyle had pronounced it sufficient "to convince any reasonable man that the matter is not one which can be readily dismissed." Objections to his findings he had angrily brushed aside. Thus, ironically, the the creator of Sherlock Holmes had been guilty of methods which the great detective would have been the first to deplore.

But this only emphasized the emotive passion which Conan Doyle had brought to his study of the supernatural. Was it, I wondered, the result perhaps of an unconscious effort to prove that Charles and his preoccupation with the nether world had not simply been the outpourings of a senile failure but sensitive work of some value and significance—the product, in fact, of a "developed spirituality"? I couldn't tell for sure since Conan Doyle had nowhere explained his commitment to fairies, but more far-fetched theories than this had been put forward and the link between father and son in this area remained a striking one at the very least. It was not, perhaps, evidence which Holmes would have put much store by. Yet he would have had to acknowledge that Conan Doyle was singularly discreet about his father. "I am sure," Arthur had concluded in *Memories and Adventures*, "that Charles

A debunking review of Arthur's Coming of the Fairies (1922) *from an American magazine, complete with three of the Cottingley fairy photographs reproduced in the book.*

Arthur's belief in fairies was viewed with enormous skepticism on both sides of the Atlantic, as witnessed by this satirical cartoon which appeared in Punch (*May, 1926*).

Doyle had no enemy in the world, and that those who knew him best sympathized most with the hard fate which had thrown him, a man of sensitive genius, into an environment which neither his age nor his nature was fitted to face." No epitaph could have hinted so openly at things unspoken. The mystery deepened.

Matters had now reached a pass where undiluted reasoning alone was helpless without greater knowledge. It was no admission of defeat. I recalled that Holmes, too, had often reached a similar stage in his investigations. Stuck for new clues which might bring about a breakthrough in his case, he would suddenly be galvanized into a frenzy of activity and, donning perhaps the disguise of a tramp or cabbie, would rush down the stairs of No. 221B into the crowded London thoroughfares, dragging a protesting Watson at his heels. It was time for me to take similar action. In the present instance a disguise was hardly necessary, but I knew that I must make physical contact with Charles Doyle's environment if I was now to break new ground. Edinburgh was my first destination. If the man had lived and worked there for some thirty years, there must surely be traces surviving. I boarded the overnight sleeper and sped northward in the gathering gloom.

The Department of the Environment, heir to the Scottish Office of Works, were courteous and diligent but doubtful if anything would surface about Doyle in their records. In the Civil Service it was customary for the case notes of personnel to be destroyed when the subject reached the age of 85; Doyle was rather older than that by now. But what about the records of the old Office of Works? These did exist, at the

Scottish Public Records Office, most of them simply design drawings for building and renovation work and a few business letters. I was hopeful that some clues at least might emerge, for here was the colorful evidence of a lifetime's labor in architectural draftsmanship. But again the material was curiously and obstinately unyielding, existing as if in a vacuum, rudderless in a sea of details. Only one figure was thrown into the light: Robert Matheson, the chief surveyor for Scotland and Charles Doyle's superior since he had joined the office in 1849. If Matheson had had assistants working under him, there was precious little trace of them: it seemed clear that even when design work was executed by others, it left the Office of Works under Matheson's name alone. There was no obvious sign that Doyle had been connected with the drawings for the new windows of Glasgow Cathedral, although more than once annotations in the margins bore a striking resemblance to the neat pencilings in the Sunnyside book. Or was this just wishful thinking on my part? In the end there was only one definite sign that Doyle had worked with Matheson at all. His signature suddenly appeared alongside his superior's on a master sketch for the Holyrood Palace fountain dated October 1858. Perhaps this momentary departure from custom was a tribute to Doyle's exceptional contribution to the fountain, which Matheson had described in a letter as "more in the class of a work of Art than ordinary Building work."

Still, on the evidence of these records it was remarkable how single-minded in its anonymity had been such a long career. Was this simply the Civil Service living up to its traditional facelessness? Or was Doyle's job perhaps less important than others had suggested? I knew from the biographies that during his long years of service his salary had risen to a level of £250 (in 1849 it had been £180). Why had there been no corresponding promotion in terms of responsibility for a draftsman who, on the strength of the Holyrood Fountain at least, was undeniably talented? Further exhaustive researches amongst other material that might be relevant to Doyle's case failed to deliver. There was no mention of him in the Scottish Home and Health Records, which listed mental patients as well as criminal offenders and, stranger still, there was no record of his having a will or having been the subject of any other legal arrangement (although I was interested to note that Charles's eldest child Annette, who died in 1890, had willed that her estate of £420 be used expressly on behalf of her father). The persistent elusiveness of the man was beginning to worry me and, not for the first time, to prompt suspicions which went beyond his "developed spirituality."

Some of these doubts were soothed by a quick perusal of the nineteenth-century Edinburgh Post Office Directories, an annual register of addresses and occupations. This record confirmed that Doyle had worked for the Scottish Office of Works, but only as the second of, first, three assistants to Matheson and then, from 1869, four. He had also definitely resided at a number of addresses in the city. Some of these were still standing, and inspection revealed modest apartments in rather rundown blocks which had once possessed a certain grandeur, the classic resort in fact of that class of genteel poor to which the Doyles belonged. So at least the connection between Charles and Edinburgh was a concrete one.

But the directories also shed some new light upon the chronology of the case. They showed that Doyle had left his employment with the Office of Works in 1877-78 (at the same time, in fact, that Matheson retired). Thereafter he was listed simply as "artist," and between the years 1878 and 1882 he had changed address no less than three times (by contrast with only one move in the decade up to 1878). From 1883 I could find no further mention of him in Edinburgh.

This information was at once corroborative and confusing. It confirmed that Charles Doyle's life had met with some exceptional upheaval in the late 1870s and 1880s. He was after all only 46 when he retired from his job. But the Edinburgh evidence conflicted in detail with that of the most authoritative biographies: the latter had stated that Charles had entered a nursing home in 1879, yet the directories showed him still living in Edinburgh as late as 1882. Or was this simply the impression created by records which customarily registered households in the husband's name? A minor detail in itself, this discrepancy was somehow typical of the shadowy life under investigation. Could it be a clue of real value or did it only appear so, rather like Lestrade's false trails? By 1883 at any rate, Doyle had left Edinburgh for good. I knew that his wife had moved to Thornton-in-Londsdale in the West Riding of Yorkshire at this time, but where had Charles gone?

Still, a pulse was beginning to beat at last in the frail body, faint but audible. A sudden breakthrough in the case now gave grounds for hope that the patient might even come off the critical list. After the impasse of the official records, it seemed worth beginning at the end. Maybe there was life to be found in Doyle's death. What had the papers said about him, for example? There was nothing in the nationals, but a hunt through the *Scotsman* for 1893 turned up an obituary notice on Monday, October 23. This mentioned that it was nearly twelve years since Doyle had left Edinburgh (were the directories right then?), though it did not say when or where he had gone. It recorded his celebrated family and referred to his illustrative work, which it considered crude in composition but indicative of "natural genius." "Personally he was a likable man," the article concluded, "genial, entertaining and amusing in conversation. Possessed of a fertile imagination it was always enjoyable to listen to his anecdotes. He was a great reader, and was in consequence well informed. His abilities and gentlemanly manner ensured to him a cordial welcome wherever he went." This added substance to Arthur Conan Doyle's recollection of his father's more positive qualities, but its bland good-naturedness was as unrevealing as most obituaries. There was no mention whatsoever of a mental institution, for instance, simply his death at Dumfries.

A death must mean a death certificate, and the Edinburgh Records Office obliged. It was the first piece of evidence to turn up something new. Doyle, the document revealed, had died at four in the morning on October 10, 1893, in the Crighton Royal Institution, Dumfries. Cause of death was given as epilepsy of "many years" standing.

Another discovery followed close on the heels of the first, appearing almost to challenge it. Searches in the records of the Scottish Commission for Ancient Monuments, which included many of the old mental asylums on its lists of preserved

Doyle's Sunnyside, a photograph of the asylum's hospital circa 1900. The view is exactly as Doyle depicted it on page 64 of the diary.

buildings, revealed that only one such institution contained a Sunnyside House. It was not Crighton Royal, but Montrose Royal Lunatic Asylum. The identity of Sunnyside was out. By matching up photographs of the asylum taken in about 1900 with Doyle's drawings of the Sunnyside building (page 64) and another tall, high-gabled block fancifully decked with dancing sprites (page 75), I was able to confirm the discovery.

A chink in the blind had opened. It began to look as if Doyle's "nursing home" *was* a mental institution. And there had been not one but two asylums; the sketchbook put him in Montrose in 1889, and sometime between this date and his death he had transferred to Dumfries. But most interesting of all, Charles had been an epileptic.* This explained a lot. A man

This gives Doyle much in common with humorist Edward Lear, also an epileptic.

with his condition would have suffered severe handicaps, severe enough in any case to preclude great responsibility and to account for an early retirement. If he was subject to violent attacks with increasing frequency, he must have been little better than an invalid. Under the circumstances institutionalization would have become a necessity, and at this date it was quite normal practice to admit epileptics to mental asylums, especially if they constituted a danger either to themselves or to others.

If there had ever been doubts about the circumstantial evidence, there seemed little enough room for them now. Epilepsy fitted plausibly into the tangled skein of Doyle's disjointed life, pulling together the loose threads into a coherent pattern. Yet one question continued to gnaw at the basis of this comfortable explanation. Was epilepsy, even in late Victorian times, such a social sin that it warranted the sort of reticence which Arthur Conan Doyle had so resoundingly displayed in talking of his father's character? Was it really the reason why Charles was so unfit to face his "environment"? After all, Conan Doyle was a practicing GP and thus no stranger to squeamish details; it hardly seemed characteristic of so resolute a champion of the truth that he should demur at such a relatively well-known medical condition.

This uneasiness was not dispelled by a late find among Treasury correspondence in London, namely Charles Doyle's superannuation particulars. I had belatedly been directed to this source by the Civil Service. It was the only place where I was to come across a direct personal reference to Charles's career, and accordingly my hopes were high of a break in the deadlock. What the record revealed, however, was nothing more than a standard retirement report: our man had left the Scottish Office of Works in June 1876 as a result of a reorganization scheme; he was to receive a pension of £150 a year; and during his years of service he had never been absent from work but had "discharged his duties with diligence and fidelity." My heart sank. Nobody was giving anything away here.

Sherlock Holmes was once again to prove a source of comfort in a moment of uncertainty. It will be remembered that in *A Study in Scarlet*, the Baker Street detective was momentarily confounded when the pills which linked the deaths of Drebber and Stangerson appeared to have no effect upon the dying terrier. He could not believe that the matter was merely coincidence, and he was subsequently proved right. He took the occasion to upbraid himself for a lack of faith in his own deductive skills: "I ought to know by this time," he had commented, "that when a fact appears to be opposed to a long train of deductions, it invariably proves to be capable of bearing some other interpretation."

Might not the same be true in the Doyle case, I wondered. Epilepsy appeared to supply the key to the puzzle, yet was it mere coincidence that neither Conan Doyle nor his biographers mentioned it, or indeed that both were so conspicuously unforthcoming about Charles in general? If it wasn't, what interpretation could be drawn other than that something was being concealed more terrible than epilepsy, concealed not so much by the biographers as by Arthur Conan Doyle himself.

One thing was certain, the search was not yet over. With public records exhausted, I would now have to approach living sources and seek out private information. Two areas immediately suggested themselves: the mental asylums at Montrose and Crighton, still in operation, and the surviving members of the Conan Doyle family. Both posed a certain challenge. Doctors, especially in psychiatric institutions, are not noted for their openness about personal case histories, and usually with good reason. Even a patient as far back as Charles Doyle was still subject to the discretion of the authorities under a one-hundred-year ruling on confidentiality. As for the family, they had something of a reputation (rightly or wrongly) for jealously guarding the good name of Sherlock Holmes's creator from the snoopings of a succession of would-be biographers and other head hunters hungry to make hay from Conan Doyle's enormous and abiding popularity. Judging by the slipshod efforts of some studies of the famous author, their attitude seemed not entirely unjustified. To some extent, family and asylums were connected. If the family were cooperative about Charles and gave their blessing, it might make an approach to the medical authorities that much easier.

In the event, such anxieties proved unnecessary. Both parties were receptive and helpful. Indeed, so much so that the potentially explosive information which they revealed was quite robbed of its dramatic impact and served to reduce the very heart of the mystery to the most natural thing in the world. The family made no bones about it: Charles had been an alcoholic. His trouble was the demon drink, or more specifically "Burgundy wine rather than whisky," as one of Arthur's nephews put it. The sound of tiny pieces gently falling into place, like a distant tinkle in some remote firmament, could now be distinctly heard. An apparently casual remark about Charles in Nordon's biography about the artist's "day-dreaming and wine-bibbing" came back to mind from an uneasy rest in some recess of the brain. Quirky details in the sketchbook—"PREVENTION IS BETTER THAN CURE" (page 23) and "BEING TAKEN UP," a crude sketch of a policeman angel escorting the handcuffed artist heavenward (page 60)—suddenly shone with new meaning. So this was "THE DREADFUL SECRET" (page 37).

The break in the clouds was short-lived, for it soon dawned on me that whereas the family had learned by rote this part of the script, they had forgotten the rest of it—or never even read it. Indeed, the extent of Charles's dipsomaniac proclivities had been a well-guarded Doyle secret, a taboo subject from which curious children and grandchildren had been firmly steered away. Those who might have known most, moreover, were no longer alive. Of Arthur Conan Doyle's five children from two marriages, only one now survived: Dame Jean Bromet, a former head of the Women's Royal Air Force.* Dame Jean had little new to tell about Charles, though agreed that her father's attitude to his father had mellowed after earlier hostility. Had Arthur been responsible for Charles's committal? Dame Jean didn't know, but she had a feeling, she said, that the parish priest had played an important part in running the family affairs; maybe he had taken the matter in hand. Mary Foley seemed to have known little about her husband's case, she observed.

Brigadier John Doyle, Jean's cousin, knew even less about

*The first-born, Mary, 4 at the time of Charles's death, died 1976; her younger brother Kingsley, 1917. Jean's brothers, Dennis and Adrian, 1955 and 1970 respectively.

his uncle's father. However, a rummage through his family heirlooms uncovered a couple of interesting items. One was a rare photograph of Charles (the only other one which has ever come to light was reproduced in the Dickson Carr biography). It was an intriguing find, for it showed a tall man with a long beard, top hat in hand, elegantly dressed, slim, almost sharp in appearance. It was dated 1865, and his hand rested on the shoulder of a young boy, the 6-year-old Arthur, according to the brigadier (see Frontispiece). This would have put Charles in his thirties at the time—over ten years before his retirement, in fact. If he was already an alcoholic by this date, he was certainly not the down-and-out type. "He had a charm of manner and a courtesy of bearing which I have seldom seen equalled," had been Arthur's words. The photo amply bore out this judgment. The other item which intrigued me was a simple birthday diary presented to Arthur's elder sister Lottie (Caroline) by their uncle Dicky Doyle. This gave out nothing of any importance to the case, but a poignant entry on October 10, 1893, caught my eye: "Papa died this day." There was no further comment.

All the modern Doyles possessed a considerable number of Charles's watercolors, some of them quite large paintings and framed. All bore the distinctive Charles Doyle imprint, delicate in style, with pale blue wash skies, winking with a quiet humor and pathos at the observer. Elves and fairies predominated. A good many of the individual drawings had evidently been torn from books like the Sunnyside one, and another of Dame Jean's cousins (on the Foley side) possessed two volumes identical in appearance to the Montrose book, one

dated 1886, the other 1888. Were these perhaps some of Charles's "many Vols . . . of not serious work"?

What was curious was that almost every surviving member of the family had some connection with the armed forces, not least Dame Jean herself. All the men were either majors or brigadiers. This was no doubt partly in the tradition of Arthur Conan Doyle's own strong military connections. The writer had served in the Boer War, had written histories of it and the First World War, and was an influential advocate of important military reforms. Had then the artistic strain, so marked in Conan Doyle and his forebears, petered out? Titles were deceptive, for the traditional military stereotype could not have had less in common with these mild and courteous descendants of Charles Doyle and Mary Foley. It was impossible when meeting Major Innes Foley, for instance, not to feel a strange sensation of familiarity, as if one was in the very presence of Charles himself. All those qualities which had come to distinguish the artist—dreaminess, courtesy, charm, a playful wit—were here embodied in this most unmilitary of majors. And what was more, the man was an expert water-colorist whose fondness for Doyle's works proclaimed itself in his own paintings, many of them on naturalistic subjects. By all accounts, Major Foley's pictures sold well, but painting was only a sideline. His real job was now, in his later years, looking after mentally handicapped adults. It seemed as if the wheel had come full circle. A poignant irony indeed.

As Dr. Watson would have known only too well, there comes a point in the recovery of some patients where signs of improvement should be a cause for greater, not less, concern, for it is at just such a point that a relapse is most likely to occur. The case of Charles Doyle proved to be no exception. A complication now arose in his condition. The family had in its possession typescripts of a few letters which had passed between Dicky and Charles in the early 1850s. These mostly contained news of Dicky's busy social life in London, with here and there mention of illustration work passed Charles's way or attempts by Dicky to use his influence to raise his brother's salary. Enough, in fact, to show that the complete family papers, last seen by Pierre Nordon in the early 1960s gave promise of valuable knowledge relating to Charles Doyle. Now came the news that all these papers were totally inaccessible. The reason for this was that they remained, and had done so for a prolonged period, as part of litigation between the widow of Dennis Conan Doyle, Arthur's eldest son by his second marriage, and the Swiss trustees of the family's literary estate. Until the suit was finally completed—which might take months if not years I was told—the papers would remain locked in a London lawyer's office and could not be touched by anyone. This meant that the best chance of plugging some of the gaps in our knowledge of Charles Doyle's life was now an extremely slim one indeed. For those who had hoped for a complete cure for the invalid, a long and patient wait by the bedside was now the only course left open.

And yet all was not lost. After all, the essential focus of the investigation prompted by the Sunnyside volume lay in Doyle's committal to a mental institution. This line of enquiry had already met with some success. The evidence of the mental hospitals themselves was now to take it a stage

further. The medical authorities at these institutions were not willing to permit an examination of their records. They were prepared, however, to give a general picture of Doyle and his condition. Crighton confirmed his epilepsy and alcoholism. When admitted there, the artist had been in the twilight of his life, almost too ill to draw anymore. Despite the verdict of the death certificate, Crighton was inclined to believe that Charles had actually died of cardiac failure—though this could have been brought on by a fit. Doyle was a private patient at the asylum, but appeared to be there on an informal basis rather than as a detainee. Fees at such places could rise as high as £1,000 a year for special privileges and luxuries, but this was far beyond the Doyle family's capacity; it is more probable that Charles was an inmate of one of the institution's detached residences, such as Maryfield, which catered for a dozen or so patients in the £25-£30 range, or Hannahfield, which housed a few elderly gentlemen "whose cases are considered chronic, and who lead there a quiet life amid surroundings suitable to their peaceful condition."*

The most revealing evidence from Crighton, however, was the fact that Charles had only arrived there in May 1892, and had come not from Montrose but from Edinburgh Royal Infirmary. So there were *three* asylums, not just two. Edinburgh corroborated this. Charles had been admitted there in January 1892 from Sunnyside, though no reason was apparently recorded—just as there had been none given for the move to Crighton. At Edinburgh he was also a private patient, paying £42 a year. He was described as a draftsman and his medical

*James Carmont, The Crighton Royal Institution, Dumfries, 1896.

records again confirmed his two-fold condition. They added that he was extremely thin, with graying hair, that he had a poor memory, and that he spent his days sketching or reading religious books. Amongst the material at Edinburgh was a letter from Charles's wife, addressed to the medical superintendent of the hospital. This spoke in affectionate terms of "my poor dear husband," but it seemed clear (as Dame Jean had suggested) that Mary Doyle knew little of Charles's condition and had not seen him for some time. The impression given was that Arthur appeared to be the member of the family most in touch with his father's case. Not for the last time did I curse the ill luck that put the family papers beyond my reach. What other pearls of information, I wondered, lay buried in that forbidden treasure trove?

And so at last to Sunnyside where, in more senses than one, it had all begun. Two points of great interest came to light here. The first was that Charles had been admitted to Montrose Royal in May 1885 from a nursing home called Fordoun House (some fifteen miles to the north), which specialized in the treatment of alcoholics. His admission had apparently been an abrupt one, following an incident at the home in which he had managed to obtain drink, had become violent and broken a window, and had then tried to escape. He was accordingly committed to Sunnyside under a detention order, though he became a paying patient. The second point of interest was that Charles's epilepsy had appeared to develop only *after* his admission to Montrose Royal: it was normal practice for mental hospitals at this date to enquire if a new patient was epileptic, but no mention was made of the condition in Doyle's case.

Why he should subsequently develop epilepsy seemed unclear, though one suggestion given was that it may have been a reaction to the withdrawal of alcohol.

The last point was a little puzzling, for if Fordoun House was doing its job properly, Charles would have felt the effect of withdrawal symptoms long before he entered Montrose. It was as if Charles was determined to maintain some last few shreds of elusiveness, a gesture on which his self-respect depended. Yet the new evidence from Sunnyside suitably vindicated the long train of deductions and suspicions thrown up by the Doyle case. It corroborated without question the fact that Charles's problems had had their origin primarily in drink, and that it was this condition, not epilepsy, which was chiefly responsible for his committal to a succession of mental institutions. Without further evidence I could not possibly tell what influence his epilepsy had had upon his circumstances. It was conceivable, though unlikely in the face of modern knowledge about alcoholism, that epilepsy had obliged him to retire and that thereafter he took to drink, making his condition irreparably worse. It was rather more probable, however, that he had started to drink heavily much earlier in his career as a result of professional disappointments which he was ill-equipped to face. Separation from his close-knit family in London and a sense of failure by comparison with their brilliance (especially Dicky's) must have only heightened his misery and self-pity. Thereafter his "problem" would have compounded his failures, to get promotion, to move back to London, to emulate his brother's success as an artist.

I felt only an explanation of this sort could account for the silences and tactful euphemisms that had been such a constant companion of Charles Doyle's shadowy progress across the pages of history. Many details still remained to be settled. When had his drinking started? How did it affect his job and his domestic life? What was his family's attitude? When exactly did he enter his first institution? What precisely was Arthur's role in the whole affair?

Still, one point was clear. Conan Doyle had known the real facts of Charles's condition and, whether consciously or not, had chosen to suppress them. It seemed implausible to me that epilepsy would have incurred the young Dr. Conan Doyle's resentment, for it was a condition which its victims could not help. Drinking was altogether another matter, however, entailing moral considerations for the Victorians, and to the young Arthur further proof of his father's weakness. Fathers and sons are rarely easy partners, and the Doyles were no exception. Only in later life, feeling guilty perhaps at deserting Charles to his lonely fate, did Arthur look to excuse his father by pinning the blame on an unkind "environment."

And there the matter had to rest—for the time being at any rate. Only now could I take off my deerstalker and put down pipe and magnifying glass, secure in the knowledge that the essential mysteries raised by Charles Doyle's case had been solved. If my conclusions seem hard on Arthur Conan Doyle, I do not intend them to be. If a man opts to ignore the true facts of life out of a certain moral squeamishness, he is hardly chargeable with conspiracy to withhold information. In the Doyle case the point is, anyway, unimportant. What the Sunnyside volume illuminates is not just a new angle on Conan Doyle, nor even the existence of a hitherto unrecognized artist of considerable talent and originality. Its real importance is as a small slice of Victorian social history, an episode caught in a sepia moment of time, as it were, affording a rare glimpse inside a particular private world fraught with ambition, conflict, disappointment, tension, anguish and disintegration.

The tale behind the Doyle book never achieves the status of a literary *cause célèbre*, nor should it be built into one. Yet its essential ingredients possess a dramatic power of almost Gothic dimensions which Conan Doyle himself would not have been ashamed to have written. But more appealing than all of this, the case of Charles Doyle projects an overwhelming poignancy. The Sunnyside book captures this spirit exactly, with its mixture of forlorn brightness, gentle wonder and anguished desperation. Part of its charm lies in its very elusiveness, its secrets and riddles requiring, like the sphinxes, no further explanation to excite the imagination. For this reason the sketches can stand alone and be worthy of interest. For those who would go further, perhaps Sherlock Holmes is their man—if they can convince him to postpone his Last Bow just one more time.

keep Steadily in view that this Book is ascribed wholly to the produce of a Mad M[an]
Whereabouts would you say was the deficiency of Intellect? or depraved ta[ste]
If in the whole Book you can find a single evidence of either ma[rk]
it and record it against me.

Charles Altamont Doyle

His Diary

8 March 1889.

I am anxious for t[...] ... this Book and any notes tha[t]
have never been sent — There are more than 157 distinct ideas in this Book

The object of all my jokes is to leave just a flavour of the solemn and have the
effect of Bitters — As far as I know both Books are quite original + whose
too big might be photographed down to workable size to fit text.

I am also very certain that any several New packs of Cards would be a prodigious Commercial
success if spiritually carried out but what has become of them all is concealed from me
22d May 1889

I am not so well I will put off writing what I was going to say till tomorrow
what I wanted to say was that I have now done a great many lots of ideas but I am kept ignorant [of]
what becomes of them — I asked them to be all sent to Mrs Doyle I understood to Publishers
as I have never had a single Book or Drawing acknowledged by her or other relatives
Can only conclude that they see no profit in them. In these circumstances I [think]
it would be better that these Books should be entrusted to the Lunacy Commissio[n]
to shew them the sort of Intellect they think it right to imprison as Mad
[...] knowledge if there is any question for publication.

WHICH IS THE PRIMEST OF THE ROSES?

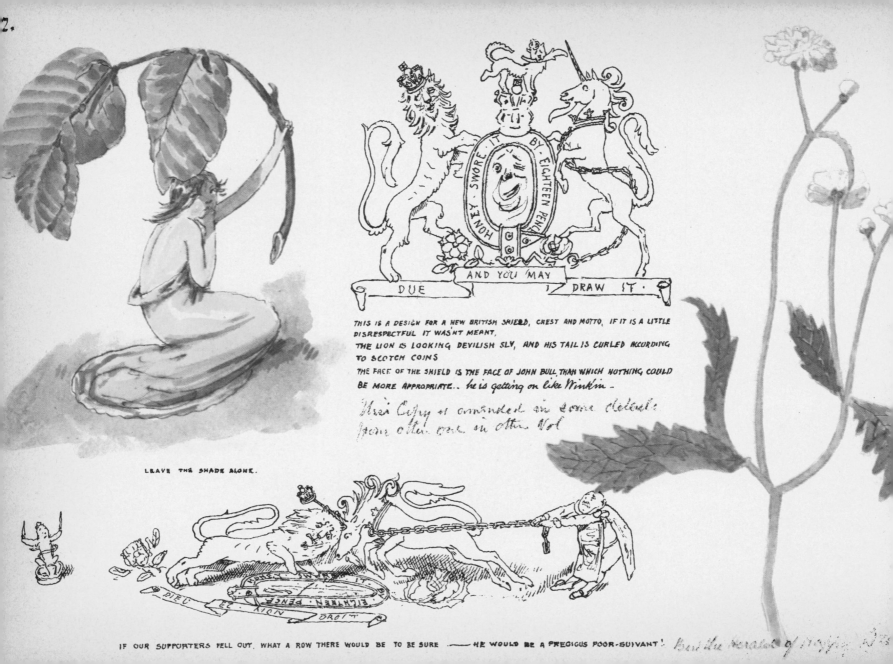

2.

HONEY SWORE IT BY EIGHTEEN PENCE

AND YOU MAY

DUE 〜 DRAW IT.

THIS IS A DESIGN FOR A NEW BRITISH SHIELD, CREST AND MOTTO. IF IT IS A LITTLE
DISRESPECTFUL IT WAS'NT MEANT.
THE LION IS LOOKING DEVILISH SLY, AND HIS TAIL IS CURLED ACCORDING
TO SCOTCH COINS
THE FACE OF THE SHIELD IS THE FACE OF JOHN BULL, THAN WHICH NOTHING COULD
BE MORE APPROPRIATE.. *he is getting on like Winkin* —

This Copy is amended in some details
from other one in other Vol

LEAVE THE SHADE ALONE.

DIEU · EIGHTEEN PENCE · DROIT

IF OUR SUPPORTERS FELL OUT, WHAT A ROW THERE WOULD BE TO BE SURE — HE WOULD BE A PRECIOUS POOR-SUIVANT! *But the verdict of maffing*

ROBBING THE ROBBER.

OTHER LIPS BUT COWSLIPS WOULD BE APPROPRIATE IN THE CASE OF PRIMROSE OVER THE WAY.

If there is confusion on this title, all I can say is that if you saw such a group you would get confused also – and probably lets lip –

A QUEER POL I SEE.

POLIDO

SNUFF

FRONT VIEW OF COCKATOO
FOR DON'T YOU SEE, ITS A COCK-A-TOES.

FAIRY'S NEST IN FLOWER POT

as much is expressed here as tens times the labour might do.

WHO NOSE WHAT A FEATURE OF GOLF THIS WOULD BE.

WITH A BIG PINCH WHAT A DRIVE YOU WOULD GIVE. –
The danger would be of the head wrenching off, and being afterwards for the other side of the hedge..

DRIVING, AND NO MISTAKE.

LET FLY
This is enough to give a feller a crick on his neck.

YARD OF CLAY

IS HE A RIBBON MAN?

17 March

THIS IS A WEEPING ASH SEEN FROM MY WINDOW, AND A CROW HAS A FASHION OF SITTING ON IT. THUS IT MAY SEEM CHILDISH, BUT IS UNDOUBTEDLY FOUNDED ON CONVENIENCE

A QUAIL, I THINK, HAS A QUERULOUS EXPRESSION

SQUIRREL NURSING THE LOST BABE

either this is a precious small Babe, or a monstrous big Squirrel —

INK-CONVENIENCE AND NO MISTAKE. &P AS HE APPEARS A HEAVY SWELL. *Truth as Death.*

5th July 1889

8

CAPERCAILZIE

EYEBROW SCARLET, A LITTLE WHITE ON WING
BREAST VERY IRRIDESCENT GREEN TINGE.   GREAT MUSCULAR POWER ABOUT NECK AND BEAK.

HOW THIS WOULD BECOME HUMANITY.

APPLIED TO A GIRL, QUAINT I THINK
WOULD HARMONIZE WITH GRAY BO

WHAT YOU OFTEN HEARD OF, BUT PROBABLY NEV
A RED HAIRED MAN.

CHINESE PRIMROSE

I think this is called a Pole Cat. It has astonishing teeth and an ill-natured look — I would'nt be rash to test the force of the teeth, on the Calf of your leg —

THE FAIRY MUSIC STOOL

ELF'S UMBRELLA

THE FAIRY CRIBBAGE TABLE

Mr Merrick London Hospital of whom the Newspaper stated "He hooked up his Trunk".

9TH APRIL 1889 DELIGHTFUL WALK AT SUNNYSIDE. WIND E.N.E.

If there was no swearing heard it was another proof of the strength of the wind.—

12.

AS TRUE TO NATURE AS I COULD DO IT WITHOUT BEING OBSERVED,

A Sketch of the Polished ways of Sunnyside.—

NOTE. THIS YOUNG PARTY SAID, WITH MANY BLUSHES, THAT SHE WOULD LIKE A COPY OF THE ABOVE,— AND SHE GOT IT. I BEING DISCREET ENOUGH TO ABSTAIN FROM ASKING ANY QUESTI

CROCUS AND CROAKER. THE MARTINS FLYING ABOUT BETTY.

knowing the drawing of the back view of a Frog's head it is judicious to hide it behind the flower. would I could hide my other deficiences!

A propos of "Dick's Journal" Copy of which Dr. Howden has kindly lent me. I should like to mention one point in the inner life of the Doyle Family this Journal was written. It is this— On Sunday the Day was observed by all the Children. Great and Small— Annette— James Dick — y, Frank, Adelaide and myself, going to the Mass, celebrated at the French Chapel at 8 o'clock A.M. This in Winter — going from Cambridge Terrace, up Edgeware Road, down George Street a Couple of Miles— often in the dark, and — ng home to Breakfast at 10 — the after day was spent in perfect Quiet till 8 in the Evening, when the Lamps were — up and more Candles were lit in the Drawing Room, and guests began to arrive, often comprising the most — ished literary and Artistic men of London and foreigners— Thackeray and Lover— Rothwell and more — lon amongst others— Most delicious Music was discoursed by Annette on the Piano— and James on the — cello till about 10 when the Supper Tray was laid— generally just Cold Meats and Salad followed — inch. We Boys all retired when this appeared— but up Stairs in Bed I have often listened to indications — most delightful Conversation till 1 or 2. It is a fact that all the political points. Extended Franchise — ition of Irish Alien Church. Vote by Ballot, &c, were then all discussed as justifying agitation— but have — since carried by Mr. Gladstone, who was then regarded as the most Conservative of Tories. At this — I heard all horrible details of the passing of the Union between England and Ireland in 1798 at the Vote for — h only Orangemen were admitted. that in itself makes the present Union quite ILLEGAL — and — the Queen were only advised as to what would be best Security for the Continuation of Her Dynasty — would now do. what she could legally do— Call a Parliament of Her Irish Subjects in — blin. to legally Vote a Union if they think wise after due Debate— or Continue to — in that City with the success— and prosperity which distinguished the former Parliament — d there.

Note. WHEN I WAS DRAWING THE ROYAL INSTITUTION; EDINBURGH, I WAS A GOOD DEAL WORRIED BY SPHINXES.

HORRIBLE FATE OF THE ARTIST WORRIED BY A SPHINX.

THE FAIRY OVER THE WAY, IS SAVING A BUTTERFLY FROM A FLY CATCHER.

Note. the Insect undoubtedly feels
the position inconvenient but it
does not know the reason why.

THE FAIRY'S WHISPER.

ANY BODY WHO HAS NURSED A BABY AS I HAVE, WILL RECOGNISE THE SMILE I THINK.

AN ANGEL TAKING A SOUL TO HEAVEN   *Easter Monday*

Mr Kinnear died very peacefully. God Bless him - If he left any moments I should like it to be sent to my wife.   many days

Charles A Doyle

18 May 1889

I should like to record my respectful reverence for Mr Forster of the John
"   my liking for Rankin's refined representations
"   my admiration for the delicious unselfishness of the
"   my affectionate remembrance of all my own Past
and a lot of other things which I mention as I put an End

THE MAN TO WHOM LIFE IS FULL OF SERIOUSNESS . —

he is a cleaner at Sunnyside who does his work seriously

ROBERT .

every touch of this was pure pallan

RANKEN'S LISTENER .

I think this is really like him — he has a good forehead

en Ireland regains her Parliament, I hope and believe her first act would be to erect a Monument to the Memory of Lord Edward Fitzgerald, brother of the Duke
Leinster, who was cruelly Murdered by Major Sirr, of the Police in 1798, while gallantly struggling for the Peoples Emancipation.
Above is suggested as an appropriate design - a Runic Cross with the Inscription indicated, the figure represents a Californian come all the way to pay his respect, 100 years hence.

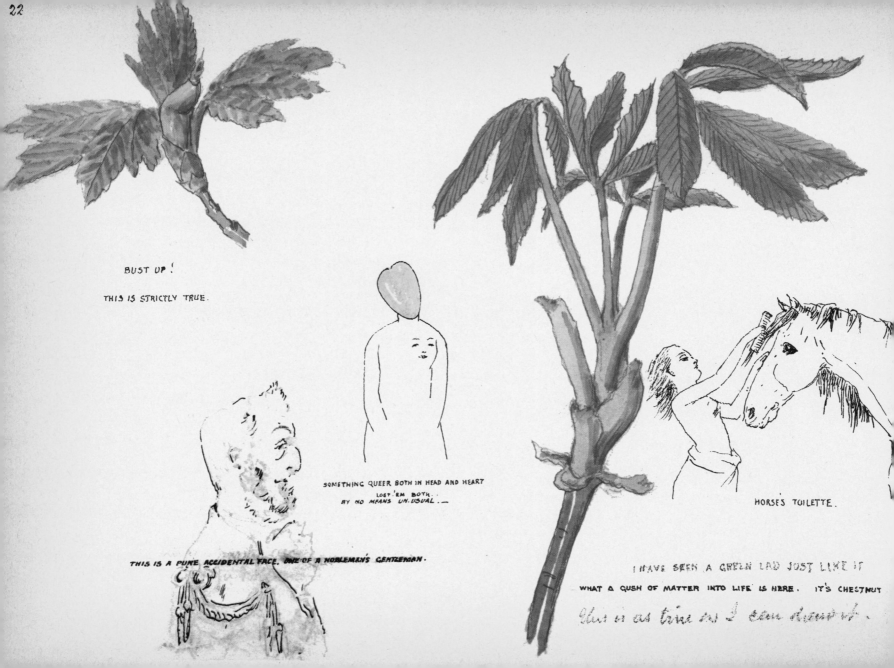

BUST UP!

THIS IS STRICTLY TRUE.

SOMETHING QUEER BOTH IN HEAD AND HEART
LOST 'EM BOTH.
BY NO MEANS UN-USUAL.—

THIS IS A PURE ACCIDENTAL FACE. ONE OF A NOBLEMAN'S GENTLEMAN.

HORSE'S TOILETTE.

I HAVE SEEN A GREEN LAD JUST LIKE IT

WHAT A GUSH OF MATTER INTO LIFE IS HERE.   IT'S CHESTNUT

this is as true as I can draw it.

PREVENTION IS BETTER THAN CURE

LET'S HOPE SHE WILL BE APPLYING HER BROOM DIFFERENTLY BYE AND BYE.

PRO.MIS —

THIS IS NOT AN OLD MISS

PRO-FILE.

NOR IS THIS AN OLD FILE.

GLIMPSE OF HIGH FLYERS

THIS WILD FLOWER WAS PICKED IN WOOD ABOVERIVER
NO APPARENT CONNECTION WITH STALK.

THE ELABORATION OF LEAVES IS WONDERFUL
THESE LEAVES ARE MUCH USED IN GOTHIC STAINED GLASS

A WILD FLOWER OF A LONDON SLUM.

THAT POPPY WAS PICKED ON HAMPSTEAD HEATH, BY TOMMY LAST SATURDAY NIGHT ...   A TWIG OF FRESH FIR

TO AN APPRECIATIVE EYE A FEW TOUCHES SUGGEST
MUCH AS THE MOST FINISHED DRAWING. AND

MINIMUM OF EXECUTION EXPRESSES ALL THAT CAN
CONVEYED BY THE MOST ELABORATE PICTURE.
THAT PENSIVE GIRL IS GAZING AT THE SUNFLOWER WH
THE DOVE IS COOING OF HOPE.

NAPOLEON III UTILIZED THE BLOT OF HIS LIFE - 2ᴺᴰ DECEMBER 1851 TO SOME PURPOSE .

UTILIZING A BLOT .

THE OLPHERT EVICTIONS.

DUNDEE ADVERTISER 18TH APRIL 1889. "THEY THE POLICE" BROKE OPEN THE DOORS WITH HATCHETS, AND ARRESTED THE INMATES, INCLUDING TWO BABIES OF 4 AND 6 MONTHS RESPECTIVELY".

Talk about Austrians in Hungary after that — you may pile up agony higher, but I can't. it is an unequal contest — whatever so...
... been no Malice. and ... ver the Austrians inflict shall be borne with as littl...

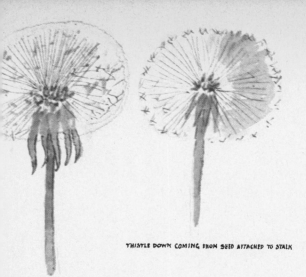

...KDOWN ENDING IN WHITE STAR

THISTLE DOWN COMING FROM SEED ATTACHED TO STALK

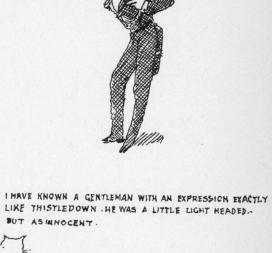

I HAVE KNOWN A GENTLEMAN WITH AN EXPRESSION EXACTLY
LIKE THISTLEDOWN. HE WAS A LITTLE LIGHT HEADED —
BUT AS INNOCENT.

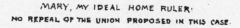

MARY, MY IDEAL HOME RULER:
NO REPEAL OF THE UNION PROPOSED IN THIS CASE.

28.

Arthur's novel "Micha Clarke".
Reviewed on Scotsman 4 March 1889
Highly favorable.
"Glasgow Herald". 16 April 188
"Mystery of Cloomber" Literary World 11 January
as follows:—

"The so called 'Occult Science' of the East has
intruded upon by Mr Conan Doyle for the Plot
interesting book. "The Mystery of Cloomber"
Forty years, General Heatherstone is haunted
an Astral Bell whose ringing constantly
him that the cutting down in battle of Gho
Shah' one of the 'Thrice blessed and Rivera
an Arch Adeptst of the First Degree, an Ela
Brither, who has trod the higher path"
in due course be avenged. The Chelas
deciple of Ghoolab, eventually appears
Scotland. and carries off the General o
a Servant. who was also concerned in
Arch Adept's fall, to their deaths in a
almost trackless Morass in Wigtownshir
Two love Stories run thro the Book — a
there are other exciting incidents of a
Strictly Natural Kind'."

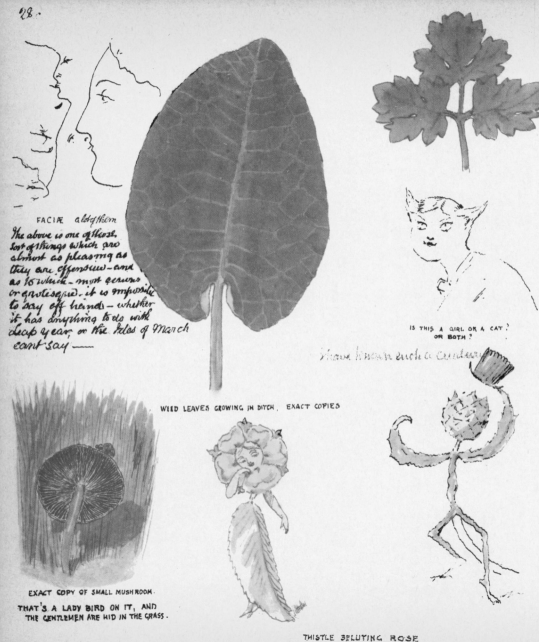

FACIÆ all of them

The above is one of those,
sort of things which are
almost as pleasing as
they are offensive — and
as to which—most serious
or grotesque, it is impossible
to say off hand — whether
it has anything to do with
Leap year, or the Ides of March
can't say —

WEED LEAVES GROWING IN DITCH. EXACT COPIES

IS THIS A GIRL OR A CAT?
OR BOTH?

Have known such a curious

EXACT COPY OF SMALL MUSHROOM.

THAT'S A LADY BIRD ON IT, AND
THE GENTLEMEN ARE HID IN THE GRASS.

THISTLE SALUTING ROSE

THERE IS AN IRISH LILT IN THIS SHAMROCK.—

A WEARING OF THE GREE

Good Friday
April 19th '89

PUSSIES

WELL IF EVER I SAW THE LIKE OF THAT

THE BIRD IS MIMICING THE ELF.

A NOSE AND NO MISTAKE

LIKE A NECK TIE
A GOOSE'S NECK THIS

CAT WAS ON A GYPSY GIRL'S HEAD

SHE AN EGYPTIAN LOOK.

MAY DAY GREETING.

THIS FAIRY IS POINTING OUT TO THE DUCK SOMETHING IT NEVER SAW BEFORE
OBSERVE THE DUCK'S DOUBTFUL INCREDULITY.

FRIENDLY CONCLAVE, BUT WHAT ITS ALL ABOUT — —

SHE'S GOT A TOOTHACE
ITS ALL VERY WELL TO SAY THAT BUT SHE LIKED IT NEVERTHELESS

30.

The Doyle Crest Motto.
This on all the Silver at home

MRS Brewster, in our hour of ease.
Well, I'll take another cup if you please-
For when a headach wringa the brow-
A miniatoring Angel. Thou-

NEXT TO Mrs BREWSTER I ADMIRE HER TEA KETTLE.

Killing Two Birds with one Stone, or rather complimenting Two Beauties with One Sketch. —

I am too delighted over to catch Mrs B's likeness

This being Easter Monday. and time to go to bed I wish to record my respectful gratitude. to the Authorities here, having a strong impression I will have no opportunity of doing so personally – and to request that my two little Sketch Books might be sent to my poor dear wife Mary – not on account of their worth but just to show who I was thinking of, and besides there are lots of ideas in them which under professional advise might be utilized – that's all I've got to say – except God Bless her & the rest of them – who I dare say all forget me now – I don't them –

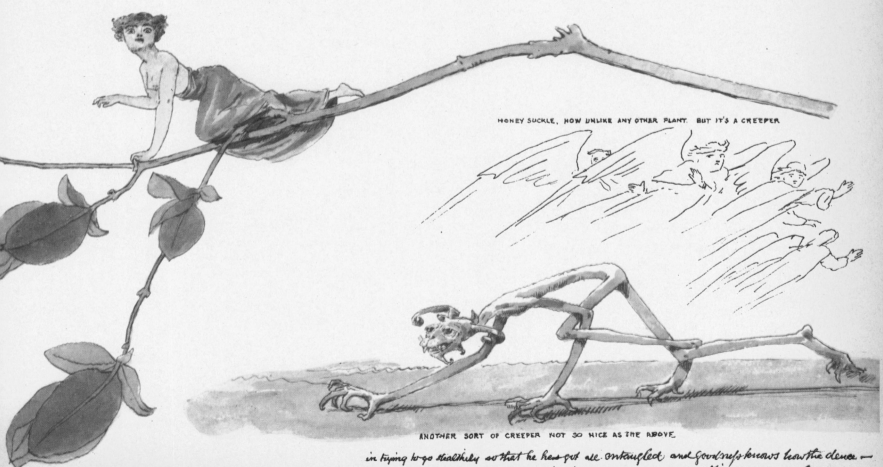

HONEY SUCKLE, HOW UNLIKE ANY OTHER PLANT. BUT IT'S A CREEPER

ANOTHER SORT OF CREEPER NOT SO NICE AS THE ABOVE

in trying to go stealthily so that he has got all entangled and goodness knows how the dence – no wonder if a feller's mind has got confused with this Fiend. and as to the angels the sooner they get away the better for themselves. –

CIRCUMVENTION

wasn't too ill to enjoy the ____ uncommonly well

MAY LIFE.   *NOT MAYFAIR LIFE.*

THIS FAIRY KNOWS A HEEP MORE THAN YOU DO.

Note. There are some Women to whom a Blot is rather becoming. but this does not aff

OF GREAT BREADTH.

EXAMPLE OF CARROTY HAIR.

S SUCH A TWIST IN HIS TAIL THAT ITS TURNED HIM RIGHT OVER.

THE DREADFUL SECRET

WHAT'S HE AFTER? YOU MAY THINK IT'S THE FLOWER — BUT — I THINK IT'S A KISS.

BOW·WOW

One of the young ladies at tea last night

"In a Girl how superior simplicity is to every other attraction"

DON'T I WISH I COULD CLENSE MY WAYS AS SHE DOES HERS!

SOAPEARIORLY—

SHE PUTS HER BACK INTO IT.

A common practice of hers—

59

" I BET MY MONEY ON THE BOB TAIL NAG, SOMEBODY BET ON THE BAY..".

40.

Wonderful effect of what the Dr gave me
at my tent a ago...

I BELIEVE THIS IS TECHNICALLY KNOWN AS A "PICK-ME-UP".

21 May 1889

THESE TWO PAGES INDUC

4'

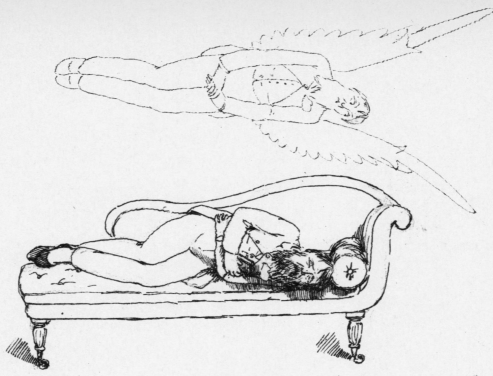

Did ever man draw himself in that Condition - his last gasp - before
what you may call drawing him close.

PORTRAIT OF A GENTLEMAN, AND YOU'LD REQUIRE TO BE TOLD SO.

the say true as Life - but this is true as Death.

R

22 May 1837

MENDOUS HEADACH.

WHAT ABOUT THE CROCODILES I DON'T KNOW, THEY M
HAVE HAD A QUEER TASTE. BUT I DON'T THINK, THE
PRINCESS WOULD HAVE BEEN BATHING, IF THEY WERE ABOU

• STUDY FOR MOSES ON THE NILE

44

DOCTORS COMMONS .

THIS COUPLE WERE OBSERVED ON SATURDAY EVENING BEHIND HERALDS COLLEGE, LONDON .

THE USE A UNICORN MAKES OF IT'S HORN WITH ITS POCKET HANKERCHIEF. IT NOSE NOTHING ABOUT IT .

here a unicorn has been known to get a bad cold in the head by wearing her bonnet on the point of his Horn

THIS WAS WHEN THEY MADE IT UP AFTER THEY HAD SUCH A ROW — SEE p.2. TO IT WE OWE HALF A CROWN. THE LION WEARING THE OTHER HALF .

IN THIS NEIGHBOURHOOD THEY GIVE YOU LOTS OF MINT SAUCE. AND KEEP THEIR COPPERS HOT. AND THEIR SALES ARE CONDUCTED BY A CHAN-SELLER, BUT YOU WILL PROBABLY BE SOLD, WITHOUT A CHANCE, YOUR FLINT BEING FIXED WHILE THEY CALL IT A BUDGE-IT.

WHICH SEEMS A LITTLE INCONSISTENT .

HONI SOIT QUI MAL PENCE

HOW THE ROYAL ARMS LOOK AFTER BEING INSULTED .

YOUR TRUE UNION JACK .

OBSERVE THE TERRIFIC WINK HE'S INDULGING IN .

THE IRISH HARP .

OU SEE ITS QUITE A MISTAKE TO APPLY THE TERM 'WASPISH' TO WHAT'S UNCIVIL. THIS CREATURE IS POLITE..

46.

WHAT AN IRISHMAN WAS, AND IS ALWAYS BELIEVED TO BE UNDER BRITTISH RULE.   WHAT THE IRISHMAN CERTAINLY IS UNDER AMERICAN RULE

TELL US THE REASON WHY ?.

47.

NOTE. That Book he has got is called the "Ursuline Manual, and has been his best friend. The Ursulines are a community of Nuns in Ireland where this valuable Book was compiled.

7th June 1889

come home.

48

GLORIA IN EXCELSIS EO

et · in · terra · pax
hominibus ·
bonæ · voluntatis

AMEN

24th June 1889.

CHRISTMAS AND MAY

52.

ON THE OUT LOOK.

THE HERALDS AND POURSUIVANTS MARCHING FROM EDINBURGH CASTLE TO THE HIGH STREET CROSS TO MAKE PROCLAMATION OF THE MEETING OF PARLIAMENT.

MADAM

DAM MAD.

QUITE THE REVERSE

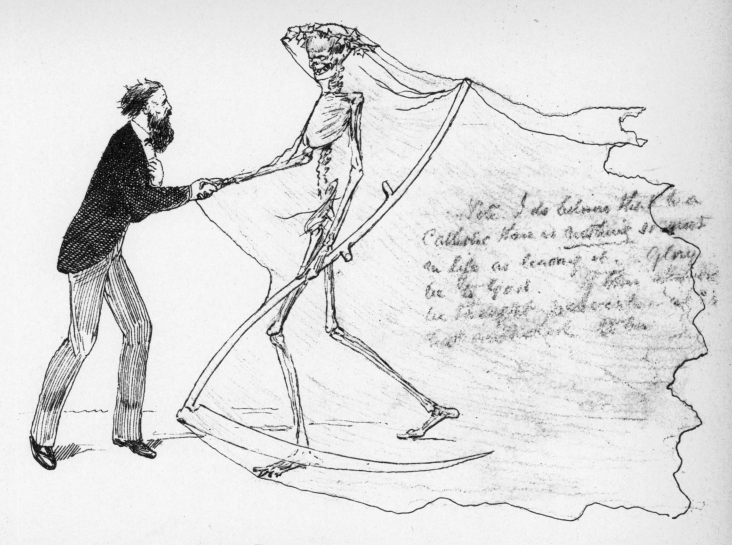

WELL MET.

56.

I am certain if my many Vols of, well, I'll say of not serious Work, were organised into some form submittable to the Ps they would tickle the taste of innumerable men like myself – and be the Source of much Money which I should like to bestow on my Daughters, but Imprisoned under most depressing restrictions, what can I do? –

I believe I am branded as Mad solely from the narrow Scotch Misconception of Jokes – If Charles Lamb or Tom Hood had been caught, they would have been treated as I am, and the latter would probably have never written "the Song of a Shirt" –

In compiling a Book of this Sort, a great deal consists in the knack of not saying too much, nor by saying too little leaving any doubt as to the point, tho' in some cases the point is best gained by raising a doubt – Nor is it only in this Book that such is the case – Many Cases are definitely Settled only by the force of the Doubt expressed, as many things are best expressed by stating what they are not – as for instance my claim for Sanity is not best made by enlarging on my common sense – as in the possession of a certain Class of ability demonstrated in this Book and proved by 30 Years of Official Public Life, tho' unfortunately not seen by certain Members of my own Family – I would have thought however, that it would be the duty no less than the pleasure of refined Professional Gentlemen to protect men like myself – than otherwise – and not endorse utterly false conception of sanity or Insanity to the detriment of the life and liberty of a harmless Gentleman – ———

Thistle leaf shewing Bluish Colour of back –

5th June 1889.

KISSING A SPHINX

I DARE DO A GOOD DEAL IN THIS LINE _ BUT REALLY _

"There were Giants in those days" quotation.

BRITANIA'S MORNING RIDE WHEN IN EGYPT.

NOTE. THAT HERRING THO' CAUGHT IN THE RED SEA, WAS NOT A RED ONE ITSELF.

3. Did you notice the Sycamore
come sailing down the Stream
O Did you notice the Sycamore
come sailing down the St

Then pass your half arount
So also keep your hearts he
and a glass of good liqu
Will do as all human.

And if we live another year
What jolly brave boys we'll

"Old English Ballad

TRACING OF SICAMORE.

IN DOING THIS I TURNE OVER A NEW LEAF AND NO MISTAKE.

ALTHO' ITS SICAMORE, DRAWING MORE OF IT WOULD MAKE ANY ONE SICKER.

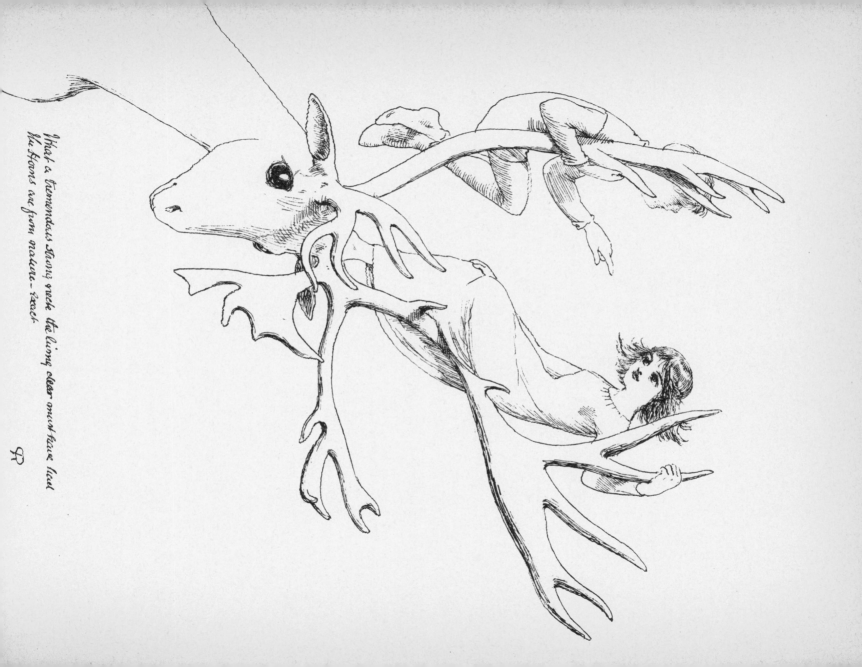

What a tremendous strong neck the living dear must have had
the horns are from nostril reach

60.

NOTE. There is one of the attendant Girls in a bluish plate dress, and the brightest Scarlet Stockings, — if she only knew how it became her — She'd —

A DEER HUNT AND NO MISTAKE.

BEING TAKEN UP

A DEAR HUNT, AND GREAT MISTAKE

19 July 1859

NEXT HER HEAD

SUNNYSIDE PICNIC, 6TH JUNE 1889. AND ANY NICER SANDWICHES AND BEER I NEVER MET, AND TRIED TO PROVE.

f GROWING UNDER HEDGE FOLDED SHARPLY AS SHEWN . .

The Fairies make a Hood of it

This is the origin of Hood winking
·le would only make the shapes and colours
nary tree leaves a Study. they would open
new happiness and profitable resource,
·ggestion of form.

How a Sprig of Fir would
replace a feather.

A NEW BRANCH OF HAIRDRESSING

PHOTON (?) ADDITIONS TO SUNNYSIDE ASYLUM

Small groups will afterwards a Settled Scene.

4th July 1882

In Centre of Dining Table at Sunnyside
what adventitious Scraps their recals to my Memory

AP

7 June 1887

WHERE PUSSY USED TO SIT AT HOME
OBSERVE HER OBSERVANT CRITICAL LOOK, FRIENDLY BUT SORROWFUL.

AMENITIES OF POLITE SOCIETY AS EVERY MORNING CONDUCTED IN THE DORMITORY OF SUNNYSIDE
WEEN MR FREDERICK AND HIS MOST OBEDIENT SERVANT.

JST SEEN THIS OUT OF THE WINDOW, COULD UNSELFISHNESS GO FURTHER?

TENDRIL PENDING FROM PLANT IN HANGING FLOWER POT AT SUNNYSIDE

Saluting Miss May. Blossom's her name —

Sorry I had no Cobalt but had to use raw Prussian Blue.

7th March 1887

A Subject of this character is intended for a fire Screen — on a Winter morning it would be suggestive & the bright Green refresh the Eye.

If this night of Bones should be any last. then my last expressed wish God bless my Wife Mary and my dear Children

Charles Altamonte Doyle

THIS

BUSTING OUT.

THIS LIT

TRYING TO GET OUT OF QUOD

HURRAH!

SUCCEDED

18th July 188

74

never suspected the *brute* would have played me this trick but you see it is all cunning – the effect is, however, good I think

STOP THIEF!

LOST LABOUR.

REAR ATTACK

IF YOU FELT THIS YOU WOULD BE ASTONISHED WHAT IT MEANT —

FRONT ATTACK

ONE IN HIS BREADBASKET

If this transaction is accomplished by a strong man stealing up behind a small man and letting fly it is smiled at by Society as legitimate warfare – but if this

is done it is denounced as unfair.

76.

THE CLOSE EMBRACE.

18th July 1889.

JULY 1889 THO' DRAWN AT AN EARLIER DATE
THE ACTUAL ACCOMPLISHMENT OF THE EVENT IS TODAY
I BELIEVE.

Charles Altamont Doyle

SCOTCHMEN ENJOYING HIGHLAND SCENERY. A fact.

The sheep were astonished at them and no wonder — but observe the silent disgust of their Guardian angels

6th June 1889 —

THE EVIDENCE TRANSCRIBED

FOLLOWING IS A page by page transcription of the words of Charles Doyle, as they appear in the diary. In an effort to recreate something of the spirit and flavor of the annotations, Charles's spelling, capitalization and punctuation have been retained and line breaks clearly indicated. Annotations made by Doyle in pencil have been appropriately labeled; all other annotations are in ink.

NOTE: Careful readers will undoubtedly observe the two variant spellings of Charles's middle name that occur in the diary, most noticeably on the opening page where he signs himself "Charles Altimonte Doyle." It is unclear why Charles writes "Altimonte" here rather than "Altamont," the spelling that appears in official records. Perhaps it is simply a rather self-conscious gesture on his part, in tune with the substitution of the Scottish-sounding "Buke" for "Book." Perhaps also some pun is intended. "Altimont" is the other variation that occurs.

FRONTISPIECE
Top Left
Charles Altimonte Doyle
    His Buke
        8 March 1889.

Above Right: Pencil annotation
keep steadily in view that this Book is ascribed wholly to the produce of a MADMAN / Whereabouts would you say was the deficiency of intellect? or depraved taste / If in the whole Book you can find a single Evidence of either, mark / it and record it against me.

Below: Pencil annotation
I am anxious for this[?] [*middle portion of line obliterated*] the other Book and any Notes that / have ever been [*word indecipherable*] — There are more than 167 distinct Ideas in this Book / The object of all my jokes is to leave just a flavour of the solemn and have the / effect of Bitter—As far as I know both Books are quite original— & where / too big might be photographed down to bookable size to fit text.

I am also very certain that my several New packs of Cards would be a prodigious Commercial, / success if spiritedly carried out— but what has become of them all is concealed from me.
                                                22nd May 1889.

I am not—well I will put off writing what I was going to say— till tomorrow— / what I wanted to say was that I have now done a great many Vols. of ideas—but I am kept ignorant of / what becomes of them. I asked them to be all sent to Mrs. Doyle and submitted to Publishers, but / as I have never had a single Book or Drawing acknowledged by her or other relatives I / can only conclude that they see no profit in them. In these circumstances I think / it would be better that these Books should be entrusted to the Lunacy Commissioners / to show them the sort of Intellect they think it right to Imprison as Mad & / let them judge if there is any question for publication.

PAGE 1
WHICH IS THE PRIMEST OF THE ROSES?

Bottom Right: Very faint pencil annotation
Who Ever saw a Tortoise with a Loving look before?

PAGE 2
Top Row, Left
LEAVE THE SHADE ALONE.

Top Row, Center
THIS IS A DESIGN FOR A NEW BRITISH SHIELD, CREST AND MOTTO, IF IT IS A LITTLE / DISRESPECTFUL IT WAS'NT MEANT, / THE LION IS LOOKING DEVILISH SLY, AND HIS TAIL IS CURLED ACCORDING / TO SCOTCH COINS / THE FACE OF THE SHIELD IS THE FACE OF JOHN BULL, THAN WHICH NOTHING COULD / BE MORE APPROPRIATE.—he is getting on like Winkin'—

Pencil annotation below:
This Copy is amended in some details / from other one in other Vol.

Bottom Row, Left
IF OUR SUPPORTERS FELL OUT, WHAT A ROW THERE WOULD BE TO BE SURE——HE WOULD BE A PRECIOUS POOR-SUIVANT!

Bottom Row, Right: Pencil annotation
Best the Herald of Happy Days!

PAGE 3
ROBBING THE ROBBER.

PAGE 4
Top Left
OTHER LIPS BUT COWSLIPS WOULD BE APPROPRIATE IN THE CASE OF PRIMROSE OVER THE WAY.
If there is confusion in this title, all I can say is that if you saw such a group you would get confused also— / and probably lets lip—

Top Right: 2 drawings
A QUEER POL I SEE.   POLIDORE.

Center Row, Left to Right
FAIRY'S NEST IN FLOWER POT

as much is expressed here as ten times the labour might do—

FRONT VIEW OF A COCKATOO
FOR DONT YOU SEE, IT'S A COCK-A-THREE.

WHO NOSE WHAT A FEATURE OF GOLF THIS WOULD BE.
WITH A BIG PINCH WHAT A DRIVE YOU WOULD GIVE.—
The danger would be of the head wrenching off, and being afterwards found on / the other side of the hedge.—

Bottom Row, Left to Right
DRIVING, AND NO MISTAKE.

LET FLY
This is enough to give a feller a crick in his neck.

YARD OF CLAY

Pencil annotation below:
IS HE A RIBBON MAN?
          17 March 1889.

PAGE 6
Top Left
THIS IS A WEEPING ASH SEEN FROM MY WINDOW, AND A CROW HAS A FASHION OF SITTING ON IT THUS / IT MAY SEEM CHILDISH BUT IS UNDOUBTEDLY FOUNDED ON CONVENIENCE

Bottom Left
A QUAIL, I THINK, HAS A QUERULOUS EXPRESSION

Bottom Right
SQUIRREL NURSING THE LOST BABE
either this is a precious small Babe, or a monstrous big Squirrel—

PAGE 7
Left to Right
INK-CONVENIENCE AND NO MISTAKE.

℟ AS HE APPEARS A HEAVY SWELL.

Truth as Death.

Pencil annotation above:
You may say what you like / but there is power on the
[*word indecipherable*]

5th July 1889

PAGE 8
Top Left
CAPERCAILZIE

EYEBROW SCARLET, A LITTLE WHITE ON WING / BREAST VERY
IRRIDESCENT GREEN TINGE. GREAT MUSCULAR POWER ABOUT NECK
AND BEAK.

Right, Top to Bottom
HOW THIS WOULD BECOME HUMANITY.

APPLIED TO A GIRL, QUAINT I THINK.
WOULD HARMONIZE WITH GRAY BONNET.

WHAT YOU OFTEN HEARD OF, BUT PROBABLY NEVER SAW, A RED
HAIRED MAN.

PAGE 9
CHINESE PRIMROSE.

PAGE 10
I think this is called a Pole Cat. He has astonishing teeth and an
illnatured look— / It wouldn't be nice to test the force of the teeth
in the Calf of your leg—

PAGE 11
Top row, left to right
THE FAIRY MUSIC STOOL

ELF'S UMBRELLA

Mr Merrick, London Hospital of whom / the Newspaper stated "He
hooked up his trunk."

THE FAIRY CRIBBAGE TABLE

Bottom row
9th APRIL 1889 DELIGHTFUL WALK AT SUNNYSIDE WIND E.N.E.
NOTE. If there was no swearing heard it was another proof of the
strength of the wind.—

PAGE 12
Top
Note What a delicious little romance this opens up. When HE
gets his Copy how proud he will be of his industrious, useful Girl /
and his Mother will think to herself how clean she looks.—

Center
AS TRUE TO NAUTRE AS I COULD DO IT WITHOUT BEING OBSERVED.

Bottom
A Sketch of the Polished ways of Sunnyside—
NOTE. THIS YOUNG PARTY SAID, WITH MANY BLUSHES, THAT SHE
WOULD LIKE A COPY OF THE ABOVE,—AND SHE GOT IT. I BEING
DISCREET ENOUGH TO ABSTAIN FROM ASKING ANY QUESTIONS—

PAGE 13
CROCUS AND CROAKER. THE MARTINS FLYING ABOUT BETTY.

not knowing the drawing of the back view of a Frog's head it is
judicious to hide it behind the flower—would I could hide my other
deficiencies!

PAGE 14
Top Left
NOTE. Is it possible to conceive a Blind Worm wearing specs?
one would'nt think it, but there is a surprizing quantity of Drawing,
just on the beak of a Magpie.

Top Right
GET AWAY AND LEAVE MY POOR BLIND WORM ALONE

PAGE 15
Top

A propos of "Dick's Journal"—Copy of which Dr. Howden has kindly lent me—I should like to metion one point on the inner / life of the Doyle Family when this Journal was written—It is this—On Sunday the Day was observed by all the Children—Great and Small—Annette—James, Dick / Henry, Frank, Adelaide and myself, going to the Mass, celebrated at the French Chapel at 8 o'clock A.M. This in Winter /meant going from Cambridge Terrace, up Edgeware Road—down George Street a Couple of Miles—often in the dark, and / getting home to Breakfast at 10— The after day was spent in perfect quiet till 8 in the Evening when the Camphore / Lamp and Mole Candles were lit in the Drawing Room, and guests began to arrive, often comprizing the most / distinguished Literary and Artistic Men of London and Foreigners —Thackery and Lover—Rothwell and Moor / Sculptor amongst others—Most delicious Music was discoursed by Annette on the Piano—and James on the / Vilolencello till about 10 when the Supper Tray was laid—generally just Cold Meats and Salad, followed by Punch—We Boys all retired when this appeared—but up Stairs in Bed I have often listened to indications / of most delightful Conversation till 1 or 2. It is a fact that all the political points—extended Franchise / abolition of Irish Alien Church— Vote by Ballot, &c, were then all discussed as justifying agitation— but have / been since carried by Mr. Gladstone, who was then regarded as the most Conservative of Tories. At this / time I heard such horrible details of the passing[?] of the Union between England and Ireland in 1788 at the Vote for / which only Orange- men were admitted—that in itself makes the present Union quite Illegal—and / if the Queen were only advised as to what would be best Security for the Continuation of Her Dynasty / she would now do—what she could legally do—Call a Parliament of Her Irish Subjects in / Dublin—to legally Vote a Union if they think wise after due Debate—or Continue to / sit in that City with the success —and prosperity which distinguished the former Parliaments / held there.

Bottom Left
HORRIBLE FATE OF THE ARTIST WORRIED BY A SPHINX.

Right
NOTE. WHEN I WAS DRAWING THE ROYAL INSTITUTION, EDINBURGH, I WAS A GOOD DEAL / WORRIED BY SPHINXES.

PAGE 16
Top Left
THE FAIRY OVER THE WAY, IS SAVING A BUTTERFLY FROM A FLY CATCHER.

Pencil annotation below
Note. This Insect undoubtedly feels / the position inconvenient but it / does not know the reason why.

Below, Center
THE FAIRY'S WHISPER.

Below, Left
ANY BODY WHO HAS NURSED A BABY AS I HAVE, WILL RECOGNISE THE SMILE I THINK.

PAGE 18
Top to Bottom: All annotations in pencil
AN ANGEL TAKING A SOUL TO HEAVEN.   Easter Monday

Mr Kinnear [?] Died very peacefully—God Bless him—If he left any Momento I / should like it to be sent to my wife Mary Doyle.
Charles A. Doyle
13 May 1889

I should like to record my respectful reverence[?] for Mrs. Brewster
at the [2 words indecipherable]
„ my liking for Rankin's refined expression
„ my admiration for the delicious Mrs. [word indecipherable] and Family
„ my affectionate remembrance of all my own Family and a lot of other things which something is [next 4 words indecipherable] put an End to[?]

PAGE 20
Top Left
THE MAN TO WHOM LIFE IS FULL OF SERIOUSNESS.—

Pencil annotation:
he is a cleaner at Sunnyside who does his Work earnestly

Below Left
ROBERT

Pencil annotation:
every touch of this was from Nature

Below Right
RANKEN'S LISTENER.

Pencil annotation:
I think this is really like him—he has / a good forehead—

PAGE 21
When Ireland regains her Parliament, I hope and believe Her first Act would be to erect a Monument to the Memory of Lord Edward FitzGerald, brother of the Duke / of Leinster, who was cruelly Murdered by Major Sirs[?], of the Police in 1798,—while galantly struggling for the People's Emancipation.—

The above is suggested as an appropriate design—A Runic cross with the Inscription indicated, the Figure represents a Californian come all the way to pay his respects, 100 years hence.

PAGE 22
Left, Top to Bottom
BUST UP!
THIS IS STRICTLY TRUE.

SOMETHING QUEER BOTH IN HEAD AND HEART
　　　LOST 'EM BOTH.
　　BY NO MEANS UN.USUAL.—

THIS IS A PURE ACCIDENTAL FACE. ONE OF A NOBLEMAN'S GENTLEMAN.

Right, Top
HORSE'S TOILETTE

Right, Bottom
WHAT A GUSH OF MATTER INTO LIFE IS HERE. IT'S CHESTNUT

Pencil annotations, above and blow
I HAVE SEEN A GREEN LAD JUST LIKE IT

This is as true as I can draw it.

PAGE 23
Left
PREVENTION IS BETTER THAN CURE
LET'S HOPE SHE WILL BE APPLYING HER BROOM DIFFERENTLY BYE AND BYE.—

Right

PROMIS—	PRO-FILE
THIS IS NOT AN OLD MISE	NOR IS THIS AN OLD FILE

PAGE 24
Top Right: Pencil annotation
GLIMPSE OF HIGH FLYERS

First Row, Left
THIS WILD FLOWER WAS PICKED IN WOOD ABOVERIVER
NOO APPARENT CONNECTION WITH STALK.
THE ELABORATION OF LEAVES IS WONDERFUL—
THESE LEAVES ARE MUCH USED IN GOTHIC STAINED GLASS

First Row, Middle
A WILD FLOWER OF A LONDON SLUM.
THAT POPPY WAS PICKED ON HAMPSTEAD HEATH, BY TOMMY LAST SATURDAY NIGHT—

First Row, Right and Below
A TWIG OF FRESH FIR

TO AN APPRECIATIVE EYE A FEW TOUCHES SUGGEST AS / MUCH AS THE MOST FINISHED DRAWING,—AND THE / MINIMUM OF EXECUTION EXPRESSES ALL THAT CAN BE / CONVEYED BY THE MOST ELABORATE

PICTURE. / THAT PENSIVE GIRL IS GAZING AT THE SUNFLOWER WHILE/THE DOVE IS COOING OF HOPE.

Bottom Row, Center and Left
UTILIZING A BLOT
NAPOLEON III UTILIZED THE BLOT OF HIS LIFE. 2ND DECEMBER 1851 TO SOME PURPOSE.

PAGE 26
THE OLPERT EVICTIONS

DUNDEE ADVERTISER 18TH APRIL 1889. "THEY" THE POLICE "BROKE OPEN THE DOORS WITH HATCHETS, AND ARRESTED THE INMATES, INCLUDING TWO BABIES OF 4 AND 6 MONTHS RESPECTIVELY."

Talk about Austrians in Hungary after that— you may pile up agony higher, but I can't—it is an unequal contest—whatever wrong /[2-3 words torn away] there has been no Malice. and whatever the Austrians inflict shall be borne with as little / [remainder of page torn away]

PAGE 27
Left
THISTLEDOWN ENDING IN WHITE STAR
THISTLE DOWN COMING FROM SEED ATTACHED TO STALK

Center
MARY MY IDEAL HOME RULER
NO REPEAL OF THE UNION PROPOSED IN THIS CASE.

Right
I HAVE KNOWN A GENTLEMAN WITH AN EXPRESSION EXACTLY / LIKE THISTLEDOWN. HE WAS A LITTLE LIGHT HEADED— / BUT AS INNOCENT.

PAGE 28
Top Row, Left to Right
FACIAE   a lot of them
The above is one of those / sort of things which are / almost as pleasing as / they are offensive—and / as to which—most serious / or grotesque—it is impossible / to say off hand —whether / it has anything to do with / Leap Year, or the Ides of March / cant say—

WILD LEAVES GROWING IN DITCH, EXACT COPIES

IS THIS A GIRL OR A CAT?
    OR BOTH?

Pencil annotation:
I have known such a creature

Top, Far Right
Arthur's Novel "Micha Clarke"—
    Reviewed on Scotsman 4th March 1889
Highly favourable,
    "Glasgow Herald" 19th April 1889
"Mystery of Cloomber" Literary World 11th January 1889, / as follows—

    "The so called 'Occult Science' of the East has been / intruded upon by Mr. Conan Doyle for the Plot of his / interesting book — "The Mystery of Cloomber"— For / Forty years, General Heatherstone is haunted by / an Astral Bell whose wringing constantly reminds / him that the cutting down in battle of Ghoolab / Shah 'one of the Thrice blessed and Revered ones / an Arch Adept of the First Degree, an Elder / Brother, who has trod the higher path" will / in due course be avenged—The Chelas or / deciple of Ghoolab, eventually appears in / Scotland—and carries off the General and / a Servant, who was also concerned in the / Arch Adept's fall, to their deaths in an / almost trackless[?] Morass[?] in Migtownshire— Two Love Stories run thro' the Book — and / there are other exciting incidents of a / Strictly Natural kind."—

Bottom Row, Left to Right
EXACT COPY OF A SMALL MUSHROOM
THAT'S A LADY BIRD ON IT, AND / THE GENTLEMEN ARE HID IN THE GRASS

THISTLE SELUTING ROSE

THERE IS AN IRISH LILT IN THIS SHAMROCK —

A WEARING OF THE GREEN

PAGE 29
Far Right, Top: Pencil annotation
Good Friday
    April 19th 1889

Top Row, Left to Right
SOMETHING LIKE A NECK TIE
IF A FELLER HAD A GOOSE'S NECK THIS / MIGHT COME.—

THE BIRD IS MIMICING THE ELF.—

MAY DAY GREETING.

PUSSIES

WELL IF I EVER SAW THE LIKE OF THAT

A NOSE AND NO / MISTAKE.

Bottom Row, Left to Right
THIS WHITE CAT WAS ON A GYPSY GIRL'S HEAD
    HAS'NT SHE AN EGYPTIAN LOOK.

FRIENDLY CONCLAVE. BUT WHAT'S IT ALL ABOUT—

SHE'S GOT A TOOTHACK
IT'S ALL VERY WELL TO SAY THAT BUT SHE LIKES IT NEVERTHELESS

THIS FAIRY IS POINTING OUT TO THE DUCK SOMETHING SHE NEVER
SAW BEFORE / OBSERVE THE DUCK'S DOUBTFUL INCREDULITY.

PAGE 30
Top Left: Pencil annotation
The Doyle Crest & Motto
this on all the Silver at home

Center and Below
MRS Brewster, in our hour of CARE—
Well, I'll take another cup if you please—
For when a headach wrings the brow—
A ministering Angel—Thou.—

NEXT TO MRS. BREWSTER I ADMIRE HER TEA KETTLE.

Killing Two Birds with One Stone, or rather complimenting Two
    Beauties with One Sketch.—

Pencil annotation below
I am too shortsighted ever to catch Mrs. B's likeness.

PAGE 31
Top
    This being Easter Monday—and time to go to bed I wish to
record my respectful gratitude to the Authorities here, having / a
Strong impression I will have no opportunity of doing so personally
—and to request that my two little Sketch / Books might be sent to
my poor dear wife Mary—not on account of their worth but just to
show who I / was thinking of, and besides there are lots of ideas in
them which under professional advise might / be utilized— that's all
I've got to say—except God Bless her & the rest of them—who I
dare say / all forget me now—   I don't—them—

Center, Right
HONEY SUCKLE, HOW UNLIKE ANY OTHER PLANT. BUT IT'S A CREEPER

Bottom Right
ANOTHER SORT OF CREEPER NOT SO NICE AS THE ABOVE
in trying to go stealthily so that he has got all entangled and
goodness knows how the deuce— / no wonder if a feller's mind has
got confused with this Fiend. and as to the angels / the sooner they
get away the better for themselves.—

PAGE 32
Top [*referring to page 33*]
THAT'S A GOLDEN CRESTED PHEASANT OPPOSITE, THE ELVES ARE
HAVING A RIDE IN THE DESERT—BUT WHETHER THEY'LL PAY FOR
IT——

Below
CIRCUMVENTION

PAGE 34
Pencil annotation
Sorry I'm too ill to finish this
wasn't too ill to enjoy the Tea uncommonly well—   24th May 1889

PAGE 36
MAY LIFE   *NOT MAYFAIR LIFE.*
THIS FAIRY KNOWS A HEEP MORE THAN YOU DO.—

<u>Note</u>. There are some Women to whom a Blot is rather becoming. but this does not apply to life

PAGE 37
Far Left, Center and Bottom
MAN OF GREAT BREADTH.
STRIKING EXAMPLE OF CARROTY HAIR.

THIS DOG HAS SUCH A TWIST IN HIS TAIL THAT IT'S TURNED HIM RIGHT OVER.

Bottom, Center
WHAT'S HE AFTER?—YOU MAY THINK IT'S THE FLOWER—BUT—I THINK IT'S A KISS.—

Far Right, Center and Bottom
THE DREADFUL SECRET

BOW-WOW

PAGE 38
Left: Pencil annotation
One of the young Ladies at tea last night
In a Girl how superior simplicity is to every other attraction

Right
DONT I WISH I COULD CLEANSE MY WAYS AS SHE DOES HERS!
    SOAPEARIORLY—
SHE PUTS HER BACK INTO IT.
A Common practice of hers—

PAGE 39
"I BET MY MONEY ON THE BOB TAIL NAG, SOMEBODY BET ON THE BAY.—"

Pencil annotation
This was all done this 13th May 1889

PAGE 40
I BELIEVE THIS IS TECHNICALLY KNOWN AS A "PICK-ME-UP".—

Above and Below: Pencil annotations
Wonderful effect of what the Dr. gave me / at my last gasp

22nd May 1889

PAGES 40-41
Bottom: Caption running across both pages
THESE TWO PAGES INDUCED BY A TREMENDOUS HEADACH—

PAGE 41
PORTRAIT OF A GENTLEMAN,—AND YOU'LD REQUIRE TO BE TOLD SO.—

Pencil annotation above
Did ever [?] man draw himself in this Condition—his last gasp—before / What you may call "Drawing" to a close—

Pencil annotations below
people say true as Life—but this is true as Death—
                                      22nd May 1889

PAGE 43
STUDY FOR MOSES ON THE NILE

WHAT ABOUT THE CROCODILES I DO'NT KNOW, THEY MUST/HAVE HAD A QUEER TASTE. BUT I DONT THINK THE / PRINCESS WOULD HAVE BEEN BATHING IF THEY WERE ABOUT

PAGE 44
Top Left: Pencil annotation
DOCTOR'S COMMON

THIS COUPLE WERE OBSERVED ON SATURDAY EVENING BEHIND HERALD'S COLLEGE, LONDON.—

Pencil annotation
NOTE a Unicorn has been known to get a bad cold in the head by wearing her bonnet on the point of her Horn

THIS WAS WHEN THEY MADE IT UP AFTER THEY HAD SUCH A BAD ROW—SEE PAGE 2. TO IT WE OWE HALF A CROWN. THE LION WEARING THE OTHER HALF—/ IN THIS NEIGHBOURHOOD THEY GIVE YOU LOTS OF MINT SAUCE. AND KEEP THEIR COPPERS HOT. AND THEIR SALES ARE CONDUCTED BY / A CHAN-SELLER, BUT YOU WILL PROBABLY BE SOLD, WITHOUT A CHANCE, YOUR FLINT BEING FIXED WHILE THEY CALL IT A BUDGE-IT- / WHICH SEEMS A LITTLE INCONSISTENT.

Top, Right
THE USE A UNICORN MAKES OF IT'S HORN WITH IT'S POCKET HANKER-CHIEF / IT NOSE NOTHING ABOUT IT.

Bottom, Left to Right
HOW THE ROYAL ARMS LOOK AFTER BEING INSULTED.—

YOUR TRUE UNION JACK.
OBSERVE THE TERRIFIC WINK HE'S INDULGING IN.—

THE IRISH HARP.

PAGE 45
Top, Right: Pencil annotation
Saturday 18 May 1889

Below, Left
YOU SEE IT'S QUITE A MISTAKE TO APPLY THE TERM 'WASPISH' TO WHAT'S UNCIVIL. THIS CREATURE IS POLITE.—

PAGE 46
Left, Right and Below
WHAT AN IRISHMAN WAS, AND IS ALWAYS BELIEVED TO BE UNDER BRITISH RULE.

WHAT THE IRISHMAN CERTAINLY IS UNDER AMERICAN RULE

TELL US THE REASON WHY?

PAGE 47
Left
come home.

Right
NOTE. That Book he has got is called the "Ursuline Manual, and has been / his best friend. The Ursulines are a Community of Nuns in Ireland— / where this valuable Book was compiled.
7th June 1889.

PAGE 48
CUPID HELPING A GAY LUTHARIAN
THIS BRACKET AND PLANT ARE OPPOSITE MY DAILY SEAT.—

PAGE 49
24th June 1889.

PAGE 51
Pencil annotation
CHRISTMAS AND MAY

PAGE 52
ON THE OUT LOOK.

PAGE 53
Top Left: Pencil annotation [*Indecipherable*]

Right: Pencil annotation
George IV Bridge

Below
THE HERALDS AND POURSUIVANTS MARCHING FROM EDINBURGH CASTLE TO THE HIGH STREET CROSS TO MAKE PROCLAMATION OF THE MEETING OF PARLIAMENT.

PAGE 54
Left, Right and Below
MADAM   DAM MAD
  QUITE THE REVERSE

PAGE 55
Center, Below
WELL MET.

Right: Pencil annotation
Note. I do believe that to a / Catholic there is Nothing so sweet / in life as leaving it. Glory / be to God. [*Remaining 2½ lines indecipherable.*]

Below, Right: Pencil annotation
19th [?] July 1889

PAGE 56
Top
I am certain if my many Vols of, well, I'll say of not serious Work, were organised into some form submittable to the Public / they would tickle the taste of innumerable men like myself—and be the Source of much Money which I should like to bestow / on my Daughters, but Imprisoned under most depressing restrictions, what can I do?—

I believe I am branded as Mad solely from the narrow Scotch Misconception of Jokes—If Charles Lamb or Tom Hood / had been caught, they would have been treated as I am, and the latter would probably have never written "the Song of a Shirt"—

In compiling a book of this Sort, a great deal consists in the knack of not saying too much, nor by saying too little/leaving any doubt as to the point, tho' in some cases the point is best gained by raising a doubt—Nor is it only in this Book / that such is the case —Many Cases are definitely Settled only by the force of the Doubt Expressed, as many things are best / expressed by stating what they are not—as for instance my claim for Sanity is not best made by Enlarging / on my common sence—as in the possession of a Certain Class of ability demonstrated in this Book / and proved by 30 years of Official Public Life, tho' unfortunately not seen by certain Members of my / own Family — I would have thought, however, that it would be the duty no less than the pleasure of refined / Professional Gentlemen to protect men like myself—than otherwise—and not endorse utterly false conceptions / of sanity or Insanity to the detriment of the life and liberty of a harmless gentleman——

Below, Left
Thistle Leaf, Shewing Bluish Colour / of Back— 5th June 1889.

PAGE 57
Left
KISSING A SPHINX.
I DARE DO A GOOD DEAL IN THIS LINE—BUT REALLY—

Right
BRITANIA'S MORNING RIDE WHEN IN EGYPT.
NOTE. THAT HERRING THO' CAUGHT IN THE RED SEA, WAS NOT A RED ONE ITSELF.

Below, Left: Pencil annotation
"There were Giants in those days"   quotation

PAGE 58
Below, Left
TRACING OF SICAMORE.
IN DOING THIS I TURNE OVER A NEW LEAF AND NO MISTAKE.
ALTHO' IT'S SICAMORE, DRAWING MORE OF IT WOULD MAKE ANY ONE SICKER.

Top Right: Pencil annotation
O, Did You Not see the Sycamore Tree
Come Sailing down the Stream.
O, Did you not see the Sycamore Tree
Come sailing down the Stream—
Then press[?] your hats round
It will keep your heads warm
and a glass of good Liquor
Will do us no harm
And if we live another year
What jolly brave boys we'll be.

"Old English Ballad

PAGE 59

What a tremendous strong neck the living deer must have had / The Horns are from nature—Exact

℞

5th June 1889

PAGE 60

Top

NOTE. There is one of the attendant Girls in a bluish white dress, and the brightest Scarlet Stockings,— / if she only knew how it became her—She'd——

2nd Row of Captions, Center

A DEER HUNT AND NO MISTAKE.

3rd Row of Captions, Center

A DEAR HUNT, AND GREAT MISTAKE.

3rd Row, Left

BEING TAKEN UP

Bottom, Center: Pencil annotation

I hope so

19th July 1889

Bottom, Far Right

NEXT HER HEART

PAGE 61

Below

SUNNYSIDE PICNIC, 6th JUNE 1889. AND ANY NICER SANDWICHES AND BEER I NEVER MET, AND TRIED TO PROVE.

Center, Above: Pencil annotation

This very fat woman / in red shawl—

PAGE 63

Left

LEAF GROWING UNDER HEDGE FOLDED SHARPLY AS SHEWN . .

TheFairiesmakeaHoodofit

This is the origin of Hoodwinking / If people would only make

the shapes and colours / of ordinary tree leaves a Study—they would open / up a new happiness and profitable resourse / for Suggestion of Form.

Right

A NEW BRANCH OF HAIRDRESSING

Pencil annotation above

How a Sprig of Fir would / Replace a Feather.—

PAGE 64

Pencil annotations

PORTION OF ADDITIONS TO SUNNYSIDE ASYLUM

It will group well against a Setting Sun.

℞

4th July 1889

PAGE 65

In Centre of Dining Table at Sunnyside— what delicious Soups this recals to My Memory

℞

7th June 1889.

PAGE 67

Pencil annotation

Genuine Columbine

PAGE 71

Left, Top and Bottom

THE AMENITIES OF POLITE SOCIETY AS EVERY MORNING CONDUCTED IN THE DORMITORY OF SUNNYSIDE / BETWEEN MR FREDERICK AND HIS MOST OBEDIENT SERVANT.—

I HAVE JUST SEEN THIS OUT OF THE WINDOW, COULD UNSELFISHNESS GO FURTHER?

Right, Top and Bottom

WHERE PUSSY USED TO SIT AT HOME

OBSERVE HER OBSERVANT CRITICAL LOOK, FRIENDLY BUT SORROWFUL

TENDRIL PENDING FROM PLANT IN HANGING FLOWER POT AT SUNNYSIDE

PAGE 72
Top
Saluting Miss May. Blossom's her name—

Pencil annotations below
Sorry I had no Cobalt but had to use raw Prussian Blue
7th June 1889

A Subject of this character is intended for a Fire Screen—on a Winter Evening it would / be suggestive, & the bright green refresh the Eye

If this night 7th June should be my last—then my last expressed wish / is God Bless my Wife Mary and my dear Children
Charles Altimonte Doyle

Bottom Row, Left to Right
BUSTING OUT.
TRYING TO GET OUT OF QUOD
SUCCEDED
18th July 1889

PAGE 74
Top: Pencil annotation
I never suspected the Ink would have played one this trick but you see / it is all smiling — the Effect is, however, good I think

2nd Row
LOST LABOUR

Pencil annotation above
STOP THIEF!

3rd Row, Left and Right
REAR ATTACK
IF YOU FELT THIS YOU WOULD BE ASTONISHED WHAT IT MEANT

FRONT ATTACK
ONE IN HIS BREADBASKET

Bottom Row, Left and Right
If this transaction is accomplished by a Strongman stealing up / behind a small man and letting fly it is smiled at / by Society as ligitimate warefare—but if this—
is done it is denounced as unfair—

PAGE 76
Center
THE CLOSE EMBRACE
18th July 1889

Pencil annotations below
[*Date indecipherable: probably 18th*] JULY 1889 THO' DRAWN AT AN EARLIER DATE / THE ACTUAL ACCOMPLISHMENT OF THE EVENT IS TODAY / I BELIEVE.
Charles Altimont Doyle

2 pencil annotations to drawing at left and right
REQUIESCAT IN PACE.
IM ACCULA ACCULORUM

PAGE 77
SCOTCHMEN ENJOYING HIGHLAND SCENERY, A F.ACT.
The sheep were astonished at them and no wonder—but observe the silent disgust of their guardian angels
6th June 1889——

A NOTE ON CHARLES DOYLE'S WORK

Most of Charles Doyle's individual paintings and drawings are now in private hands, either in Britain or America. The Fine Art Society possesses some (they appeared in an exhibition of British Illustrators in 1967), and others can be found in collections in Edinburgh and Dublin. In the United States one of the largest collections belongs to the Henry Huntingdon Art Gallery in San Marino, California. The Conan Doyle family, of course, has a substantial collection of Doyles among them, which includes well over thirty watercolor drawings and several sketchbooks belonging to Charles from his asylum days.

His illustrative work is scattered very widely in magazines, papers, books and periodicals. He was particularly associated with the *Illustrated London News* and with children's books. The British Museum catalogue lists seventeen separate titles illustrated by Charles, many of them books with other-worldly themes (such as *Mistura Curiosa*, 1869; *Our Trip to Blunderland*, 1877; and *Remollescences of a Medical Student*, 1886) or where the keynote was on humor (e.g., *The Diverting History of John Gilpin*, 1866; and *The Book of Humorous Poetry*, 1867). He also contributed to an 1860 edition of *Pilgrim's Progress*. A children's publisher with whom he particularly worked was Waterston's Nursery Library: he illustrated *Three Blind Mice* (1883) and *The Two Bears* (1880), where the interest focuses less on the main watercolors, which are rather crude and simple, than on the drawings in the margins, some of which bear a striking resemblance to ideas in the Sunnyside book. Doyle is less at home when he has to tackle everyday realities, and his illustrations for *Coelebs the Younger in Search of a Wife* (1859), *The Long Holidays* (1861) and *European Slavery: or Scenes from Married Life* (1882)—an account of wife-beating!—are among his least inspired. It is difficult not to place his pen-and-ink sketches for the 1888 edition of *A Study in Scarlet* in the same category. However, what is striking about Charles Doyle's art—as about Richard Dadd's—is that his best work seems to have been produced in the confines of the asylum. The Sunnyside book further strengthens this impression.

PICTURE CREDITS

Grateful acknowledgment is made to the individuals and organizations who granted permission to reproduce the illustrations appearing in the Introduction. The picture sources are as follows: Brigadier J. R. I. Doyle, OBE: *frontispiece*. Stanley MacKenzie: p. XVI. Mary Evans Picture Library, Blackheath: p. XX. *The Montrose Royal Asylum for the Insane 1781-1900*, courtesy of the Montrose Public Library, Montrose, Scotland: p. XXIII. Popperfoto, London: p. XIII (*right*). The Harry Price Library, London: p. XIX. *Richard Doyle: His Life and Work* by Daria Hambourg (New York, 1962): p. XI. *Sir Arthur Conan Doyle: Centenary 1859-1959* (London, 1959): p. XIII (*left*), p. XVI (*right*).

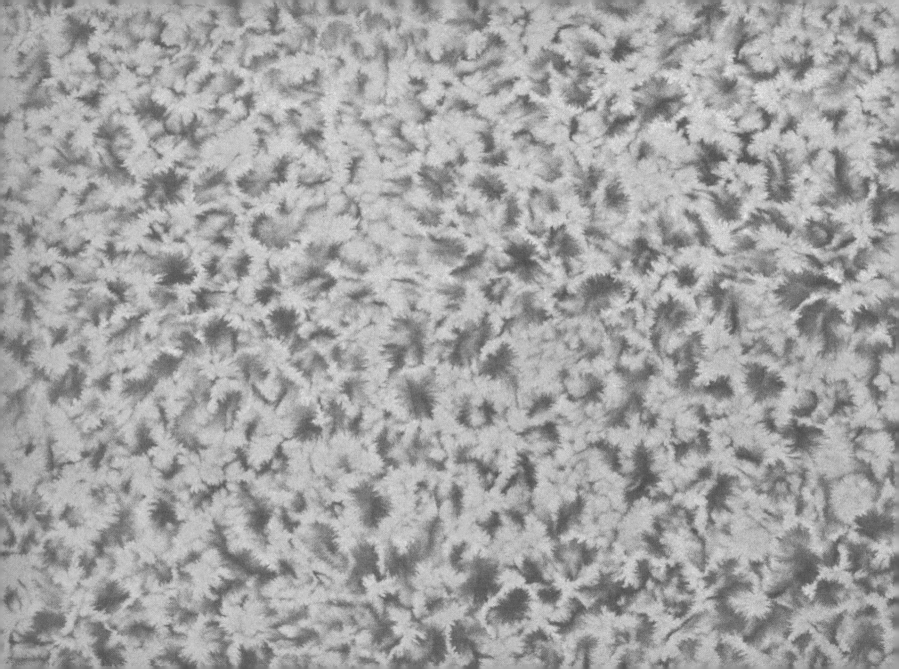

"Tigers are great," purred Jeff happily,
"but I am who I am and I love being me."
And as he washed his paws, he smiled.
It was good to be small and just a little bit WILD.

"I'll land safely on my feet!"

"And if I fall

and fall

and

fall . . .

MEOW!

"I'm good at jumping—no one can match me.
I'm nimble and quick. Even tigers can't catch me!

"I'm great at climbing way up high.
I'm difficult to beat.

But Jeff said, "No! I have to go!"
He'd had quite enough of the jungle.
He was tired and scared and missing his home.
And his tummy was starting to rumble.

He knew it was time to escape, but how?
Then he remembered what cats can do best . . .

"And now it's time that I was off.
It was really nice to meet you."
"Oh, won't you stay?" the tiger said.

"I promise not to eat you!"

"CAT!

See my stripy fluffy tail,

my tiny kitty claws.

Watch me as I pad and pounce

with my dainty little paws!"

Jeff froze! Well, how could he answer a question like that?

"I am Jeffrey Fluffy McSnuggle-Tum and I am a . . .

Jeff and the tiger found themselves nose to nose.
"What have we here, then?" growled the tiger.

The snake, looking rattled, decided to flee
when he saw behind Jeff, in the shade of a tree,
the beastliest beast in the jungle for sure.
And then, all at once, came a ground-shaking . . .

"I'm a big, strong, scary tiger!

See my stripy tiger tail,

my furry tiger paws.

Watch me as I growl and prowl—

fear my awesome claws!"

The snake was quite scary,
all scaly and green.
But Jeff puffed up his chest
and tried his best to look mean.

Jeff felt quite silly as he sat in that pool.
So he dried his wet paws and did his best to look cool.

But there in the bushes, and now wide awake,
secretly slithered a **huge, stripy** . . .

Jeff sprang into action and pounced, quick as a flash.
But he missed by a whisker and landed with a great . . .

"I'm a big, scary tiger!

See my stripy tiger tail,

my furry tiger paws.

Watch me as I growl and prowl—

fear my awesome claws!"

. . . butterfly!

The jungle was dark, and things *moved* all about him.
Jeff bravely set off to explore his surroundings!

And when something colorful caught his eye,
he couldn't resist chasing a . . .

Jeff was soon woken up by a peculiar sound.
His pointy ears twitched, and he looked all around.
His little nose wriggled at a strange new smell.
He felt a bit nervous but curious as well.

"I'm a tiger," said Jeff, "so I really don't care!"
And he slunk off for a nap in his favorite armchair.

"I'm a big tiger!

See my stripy tiger tail,

my furry tiger paws.

Watch me as I growl and prowl—

fear my awesome claws!"

Jeff sat by the window as the rain poured down,
one bored little kitty in a big gray town.
He might look small and gentle and mild,
but being stuck indoors was enough to drive him WILD!

JEFF goes
WILD

by Angie Rozelaar

KATHERINE TEGEN BOOKS
An Imprint of HarperCollins Publishers

For Jason, Leon, Matilda, and Jude

Katherine Tegen Books is an imprint of HarperCollins Publishers.

Jeff Goes Wild
Copyright © 2021 by Angela Rozelaar
All rights reserved. Manufactured in Italy.
ISBN 978-0-06-284056-1

The artist used gouache and collage when making the digital art for this book.
Typography by Rachel Zegar
21 22 23 24 25 RTLO 10 9 8 7 6 5 4 3 2 1
❖
First Edition